♥SEVEN ROMANCES♥

This is a work of fiction. All characters and events are fictitious.

These stories appeared in somewhat different form as DOOMED ROMANCE # 1-4 and KINKY ROMANCE # 1-4.

SEVEN ROMANCES

BY TOM RUSSELL

TABLE OF CONTENTS

NOTES ON GENDER

A work of fiction should not come pre-packaged with a defense, but should be able to stand up on its own, a complete universe. At the same time, in presenting these seven stories in one volume, the reader will notice certain similarities and, were I neglect to put those similarities in context, they might draw certain inferences about the author.

These seven stories were originally presented as parts of two "series", *Doomed Romance* and *Kinky Romance*. They were not "series" in the same way that my novel *Jolt City* was originally a series; there are no reoccurring characters. Rather, each romance series was defined by a formula or boilerplate, meant to quickly generate stories. Since I was only able to produce seven over the course of the last two or three years, I'm not sure how well that turned out.

In the case of *Doomed Romance*, the formula was something akin to classical tragedy. The best definition I've ever heard of a tragic hero is that what happens is completely his fault but there was nothing he could do about it. The narrators in *Doomed Romance* each have a character flaw that brings about the destruction of their romance or their loved ones.

Since that's fairly depressing subject matter, I wanted to create a companion series that would serve as its opposite; if *Doomed Romance* was male-narrated and about failure, *Kinky Romance* would be female-narrated and about success in the form of an orgasm.

All these stories, then, stick to one of these two formulae. All the male narrated stories are about destruction and misery. All the female-narrated stories are about unbridled sexuality and self-discovery. Does this mean that I think all women are sexual dynamos unable to control their urges? No more than it means that I think all men are destructive.

Though these stories all come from a generic formula, they are in the end specific stories about specific people. For every man who ruins a relationship by not letting go of the past, there are men who can mourn and move on; for every woman who enjoys getting spanked, there are many who want nothing to do with it and a few who wouldn't mind spanking somebody else.

These are stories not about "women" and "men" but about this woman and this man, about daring Rachel and melancholy Finn, plucky Elise and miserable Donald, Tuck and Gem, who are unhappy either way, that poor reptile Leon and the tormented narrator of Horny, who learns that no matter how fucked-up you are and how much you hate yourself, there is someone out there who will love you and let you love her back.

These are my people, my friends. I hope you love them as I do.

Thank you so much for buying this book.

Tom Russell, June 2009

FINN

I first met Emily while my wife was still alive. The three of us had mutual friends. We only saw her a few times, and then she seemed to drop off the radar. She hadn't made much of an impression, to tell you the truth, so we never asked about it.

I had forgotten all about her, and then about two years after the accident, I bumped into her. She recognized me first. "Finn?"

"Uh, Emily?"

"Right."

She asked how Nora was, and so I told her what happened. And then we had The Conversation, the same exact conversation I've had with just about everybody and that I've gotten tired of. Thankfully, she kept it brief, throwing in a few "hang-in-theres" and "if-you-need-to-talk-to-anybodys" before jotting her phone number down on my palm.

I had no intention of calling her. I didn't write down the number when I got home and over the course of two or three days of routine hand-washing I had scrubbed the numbers off.

A couple months later, I was just sitting around the house when I remembered a dream I had had once. In the dream, I was a huge giant, thirteen or fourteen feet tall. I had to stoop over to walk around in the house. Nora was very understanding. She helped me into the car, folded me up at night so that I could fit on the bed, tied me shoes for me so the blood didn't rush to my head, and so on. And then she was gone.

I immediately began to shrink, loses inches and feet in a matter of minutes, until I had whittled myself down to the size of a thumbnail. The house was huge and overwhelming. It took me days to safely climb down the stairs. Simple, everyday things became monumental tasks. And I had no one. Just me and this huge, empty house.

And when I remembered this dream, with no apparent reason to have done so, I was struck by an equally inexplicable urge to talk to Emily. I cracked open the white pages and found her number. It didn't look like the number she had given me. Maybe she had changed it. But I wasn't sure, and that was enough to dissuade me. I put the white pages up and went to lay down on the couch.

I was stretched out there for about ten minutes, and I went over the dream in my mind, and I wondered why I had wanted to talk to Emily. I figured that if I could figure out what the dream meant, and what had triggered it, I could figure out how it was connected to her. And then I remembered that Emily was a psychologist, and I realized that on some subconscious level I must have been aware of that. I fetched the white pages again, found her name again, and dialed the number.

She answered.

"Hi, Emily. It's Finn."

"Finn Berwick?"

"Do you know that many Finns?"

"No," she said. Then she asked me how I got this number.

"You gave it to me, remember? You wrote it on my hand."

"No, I gave you my cell phone," she said. "This is the land-line."

So I explained that I had lost the number, and that I had looked her up in the phone book. Then I explained that I had had a weird dream, and that I wanted to know what she thought of it.

"What, am I in the dream?" she asked.

"No. I just thought that you could analyze it for me?"

"What am I," she said, "a psychologist?"

"Aren't you?"

"Not the last time I checked."

"I must be thinking of someone else, then."

"Must be." She offered to analyze it for me-- "I'll do my best", she promised-- but I was feeling very embarrassed and a bit silly.

Emily volunteered that she was an emergency dispatcher, and we talked about that for a little while: different situations that had come up, people getting wigged-out on the phone, stuff like that.

"You know," I said, "one of Nora's students called 911 when she died."

"Oh," said Emily, a little put-off by my shifting gears. "I'm sorry if we didn't get there in time..."

"No. They were real quick. But they figure she had pretty much died on impact. There was nothing anyone could have done. The kid was okay, though. Nora was giving her a ride home. She came to the funeral and everything. I talked to her awhile."

"That's... that's great, Finn. Uh. So, was it a young kid, or a high schooler?"

"High school, a ninth grader."

"What did Nora teach?"

"History. She loved history. I loved it too; that was one of our common interests, one of the things that pulled us together. But I don't have the-- I'm not smart enough to really be good with it."

"Oh, don't say that, Finn."

"No, I mean, I'm not a dummy or anything. But I don't have the, uh, intellectual rigor to be a real serious student of history. But Nora had it."

"Well, I only met her the few times, but she seemed like a pretty special lady."

"Yes, she was. You know, that girl who was in the car with her-- there wasn't a scratch on her."

"Really?"

"Well, hardly a scratch. I mean, she didn't go into the hospital or anything. Had a bit of whiplash over the weekend. But Nora-- she died right like that." I snapped my fingers, though now that I think about it, there was no way for Emily to hear that. "The girl was perfectly fine. If the other car had went a little this way or a little that way, or hit at a slightly different angle, they might both be dead, or just the girl, or they'd both be alive. Funny how random life is."

"Yeah."

The conversation slowed to a crawl after that, and died a quick and relatively painless death soon after. Before I got off the phone, Emily gave me her cell again, and this time I wrote it down.

I wish I could remember Nora's voice. It was the first thing I lost. For weeks after, I left the answering machine the same. It wasn't really because I listened to it, staying up nights playing it over and over and crying or something maudlin like that. I hardly ever heard it. But I kept it there until one day I was struck by a very sudden and irresistible impulse to change it. And so I did, and I never heard her voice again.

I can remember certain physical details very clearly, but only in isolation: her eyes, for example, or the water-blister on her left prime finger, the shape of her nose, a mass of her hair. But whenever I try to bring them all together in my mind, to glue them into a face, they just kind of float there, changing shape and proportion, getting hazy and lumpy. And because of this--

because I couldn't resurrect her whole, but only in this piecemeal fashion-- I'm never really sure if it is really her that I'm remembering, or if, as I grope about for details and body parts, I'm just frankensteining her together from the lives of others. Sometimes I wonder if I still carry any of her in me at all.

Now that I think about it, I'm kind of hard-pressed to name anything that Emily and I had in common. I'm a voracious reader, while she didn't read much; she had a very passionate interest in politics, which just made my eyes glaze over; our taste in movies was, to put it as kindly as possible, severely at odds. (I'm not even going to touch on our sex life.)

But the funny thing is, at the time, it seemed to fit. We seemed to fit. Everything felt right.

A month after our first date, as her lease was expiring, I asked Emily to move in. We cleaned out her apartment over the course of her last week on the lease, moving a carload of boxes at a time and celebrating with dinner (invariably pizza, sometimes Chinese-- that staple of any new couple's diet) at what was soon to be our place.

I met her for lunch that Friday.

"I talked to Chris at work today," she said. "He has a truck. He'll help us move the furniture on Sunday."

"We're taking your furniture, too?"

"Well, yes," she said, as if it were obvious.

"Well, I already have furniture. I figured you'd just be giving yours away or selling it or something."

She seemed put off about this. "It's a nice couch, anyway. I want to save that much at least. You have to admit, it's much nicer than your couch."

There was no contest there. Emily had a nice new leather sofa, less than a year old and practically pristine. We had gotten ours as a wedding gift from Nora's aunt, who was a devout cat lady. The ratty polyester had been torn to shreds long before we got ahold of it; the cushions had lost their fluff long ago and were extremely uncomfortable.

All that being said, I was reluctant to get rid of it. On Sunday, I told Chris we'd be taking Emily's couch around the back to the side door, to the basement. Emily was perturbed, and I explained that there was no use having two couches in the living room. We'd remove mine, of course; then we'd move Emily's upstairs, where it belonged.

Chris offered to help me take out the old couch before we moved the new one in.

"No, no," I said. "I want to see if I can sell it."

"You're going to sell it?" said Emily.

"Or give it away to someone who needs it. I don't want to just throw it away, have it go to waste."

So we moved the couch to the basement, and I promised Emily I'd put an ad up about the old couch.

In some ways, it wasn't like living together at all. I worked during the day, and Emily had recently switched back to the night shift. She'd come home just after seven, and I'd have to be at work by eight. Sometimes we'd talk for a few minutes as she got undressed and I scarfed down my breakfast, but more often than not she'd come home while I was in the shower, and she'd curl up and fall asleep before I was done.

She'd sleep until two or three, and then she'd get started on dinner. By the time I got home at four-thirty, she'd be just about done with it. I was a better cook than Emily was-- a much better cook-- but if I had spent an hour or two whipping something up once I got home, that was an hour or two less that we had to spend together. I only had her until quarter to eleven. We wanted to make every second count, and burnt macaroni seemed like a fair trade at the time.

It reminded me of when I first started dating Nora. We'd spend a few hours at her place or my place or we'd go out for a bit, a couple nights a week. The entire week-- our entire life-- was structured around our dates, and because there was so much downtime in between, there was this enormous and suffocating pressure to enjoy ourselves. Everything is more dramatic when you have to compress a week's worth of affection into a handful of hours. Faults are more easily overlooked because no one wants to sour that tiny window of time together with an argument or bad feelings. You spend much of your time telling each other how much you love each other, and little else.

Once we were living together, though, we weren't under all that stress to smile and hug and be happy and witty and clever and charming. Things mellowed out, and we were able to spend more time together. Even if the conscious hours I spent with Nora and those I spent with Emily added up to be just about the same, just spending eight hours sleeping next to each other seemed to make a difference. We fell into a pleasant rhythm that was all our own.

We could be comfortable with each other, and we were allowed to be angry and pick at each other like scabs. It was okay to be petty and mean and cruel, because there wasn't going to be three or four days of separation for those ugly feelings to stew. I could always count on seeing her in a few minutes, and there was always time to say that I was sorry. That's what was beautiful about living together. About being married.

But Emily and I, we weren't really living together during the week; we were dating, and so we were always very happy to see each other and we enjoyed our time together as vigorously as possible, whether we liked it or not.

It was different on weekends. On weekends, we would spend long lazy hours together, and we would sleep side-by-side, and I would cook. And, of course, we would fight.

Just as when you're dating you save up all your love for those few brief hours that form the highlight of your week, it seemed like we saved up a checklist of faults, irritants, complaints and anger all through the week so it could explode throughout the weekend. That makes it sound bad, but it really wasn't: by Sunday night, more often than not, all apologies were tendered and accepted. And when I came home Monday we would I-love-you each other to death.

Emily loved garage sales, which is something she had in common with Nora and that I had in common with neither. I don't want to come out and say that women like to shop, but let me say this: when women do shop, much like backyard wrestling, it is done only for the sake of doing it--*Garage Gratia Garagis.*

When men shop, they shop with a purpose. I have a finite list of very specific things that I have to buy. By the time I set foot in the store, I have made out my itinerary. I go to the first thing-- boom. Then the second-- boom. Boom, boom, boom: I'm done.

I don't dawdle, I don't look at other items. And God help me, I don't look at a sales-paper to see what's on special. (I might, at times, pause to partake of a food demonstration. Hit four or five of those things and you've just had a free lunch.) The idea of strolling casually down the aisles, checking out prices here and there, and, consequentially, ballooning the damage inflicted on my wallet, does not appeal to me in the least. And the idea of going to any store without any one particular thing in mind, but just to look-- that idea drives me insane.

And that's what garage sales are: little stores with grass-and-cement floors and no roofs calculated solely to drive me insane. We have silverware, we have books, we have place mats, we have dish towels, we have comforters, and, yes, we have knick-knacks: we have plenty of all these things, and still both Nora and Emily seemed to be slack-jawed with a lust for them that could never be sated.

Generally, though, I didn't make a fuss: they knew how difficult it was for me, and so they kept their browsing time to what they must have thought was a minimum; I, in turn, accompanied them dutifully as they made their many, many, many rounds.

One weekend Emily even cut it short, and we went home after the first one. There wasn't much there, but Emily took an interest in some small paintings they had for sale. Watercolours, mostly of bowls of fruit.

"These are wonderful," she said.

I didn't agree, but I knew better than to disagree. The woman selling them was in her late thirties. "Yeah, they were my mother's."

"She bought them?"

"Nah, she painted them. She passed away last year."

"Oh," said Emily.

"I got some more in the basement if you want to look at them. I don't got no use for them."

Emily turned to me. "Finn, you want to look at them?"

I honestly did try not to roll my eyes. "If you want."

And so we went into this strange woman's strange house, down her stairs into her basement, to look at her dead mother's paintings that she was hawking for two bucks a piece. To say I was uncomfortable and irritable would be regarding me very charitably.

The paintings weren't much better than the ones in the yard. One of them caught my attention, though: a very striking young woman whose eyes were too big for their sockets.

"Who's this of?" I asked.

"That's my sister, Connie," she said. "You wouldn't know her," she added, as if I had implied otherwise.

I put my arm around Emily. "She reminds me of Nora."

"Everything reminds you of Nora," said Emily. She quickly looked through the other paintings and turned to the woman.

"I don't think I'll be buying any after all," she said. "Sorry. Thanks anyway. Your mother was a very talented woman."

"You can have them if you want," said the woman earnestly. "Don't have to pay me. I'm about ready to throw them out anyway. They're hogging up so much space. It's so annoying." She smirked, then she kicked at the painting of her sister.

In the end, we left her with her mother's paintings, and we just went home.

Emily had a sister who lived in India. Her name was Meghan and she was coming back to the states for a week so she could visit her family. She came over one Thursday night; Emily had arranged to take the day off work in anticipation. They hadn't seen each other for nearly two years.

We were introduced, and she sat down to talk with her sister while I made dinner. Over the meal, she told us about her time in India.

"I tell you, the first thing I did, soon as I got on shore?" She smiled conspiratorially at us, leaning in before blurting: "I got the biggest, fattest, greasiest cheeseburger I could find."

"I know the feeling," I said. "Nora (my late wife) went on this vegetarian kick once, which made me a vegetarian as well. I couldn't stand it."

"Well, it's alright, because I like Indian food. But every once in a while," she wringed her hands comically, "I'd get this uncontrollable urge to go cow-tipping."

"What, out of spite?"

"No!" said Meghan. "Just, y'know, to be naughty." She laughed. "I don't have any spite for anybody. I love it over there."

"You know," I said, "Indian food-- the spices and all that-- didn't start in India. All those hot spices came from over here, from the states."

"Yep," nodded Meghan.

I felt embarrassed-- felt like I was showing off or something-- and so I demurred: "Nora had told me about it."

"Speaking of not having any spite," said Emily. "Have you been to see mom yet?"

"No," said Meghan. "But I will." She shoveled in a mouthful of food and chewed it quickly. "I don't want to, but I will."

"You have to," said Emily. "It'll break her heart if you don't."

"That's assuming she has a heart to break," said Meghan.

"She difficult to get along with?" I asked.

Meghan and Emily exchanged looks and broke out into the same exact smile at approximately the same exact time. "You could say that," said Meghan.

"She's never wrong," said Emily. "Everyone else is terrible to her, but she's a selfless martyr who never makes a mistake and lives only for her children."

"Nora's mother is exactly the same way," I said. "Always criticizing. Always."

"Well," said Meghan, "we had our big break when I got my divorce and moved to India. Now," and here her voice swirled with laughter, "I should never have had a divorce. It was my fault because I didn't work hard enough. My mother, she's on her fourth marriage, but that's not her fault. She was blameless."

I nodded in recognition. "Nora's mother, she even kept it up after she died. She said if Nora hadn't been working as a teacher, she never would have went out of her way to drive the student home, never would have had the accident. So it was Nora's fault that she died. Unbelievable."

It was quiet for a moment. Then Meghan said, simply: "It's a nice meal."

I'm not sure exactly when things really went sour with Emily. One day she suggested that we break up, and we argued about that, and she started looking for an apartment. Then we'd reconcile-- it being relatively easy to do so since we lived in the same house-- and she'd stop looking. Then we'd break up again, and then we'd make up again, and so on.

Until one day, she announced that she had found a new apartment. I helped her move but we continued to date, then not date, then date again, until we just stopped dating altogether. It was a very slow death, a break-up by attrition, and when I look back on the entire life of our relationship, I guess it was that way from the start.

She never really gave me a real good concrete reason for breaking it off. Certainly there was some dissatisfaction, and we didn't get to spend a whole lot of time together. She did say that she felt neglected, but come to think of it, so did I. She said I never really listened to her, but every time I mentioned Nora her eyes just glazed over.

It's been four years now since the last time I saw Emily. I can't quite remember what she looks like. I try to hold her together but she's all jumbled up.

RACHEL

There was a young Englisher standing against the building, his hands in his pockets. He was chewing on something, smacking his lips and staring at me. He reached into his mouth and pulled the thin white mass out between his fingertips. He walked up to the buggy, smiled, and stuck the gooey substance on its side.

"Nice bonnet you got there," he said.

"Thank you," I said quietly.

"What's your name?"

"Rachel."

He spit on the ground out of the side of his mouth. "Thought you all had biblical names."

"It is from the bible." I tried not to give offense.

"Hmm," he said, nodding. "Learn something new every day." He spit again. Then he reached into the buggy and touched my white bonnet. "Aren't you going to stop me?"

I did not answer. I had said too much to him already. He repeated the question. Again, I gave no answer.

"Guess I can have this then?" he said.

"Please don't," I said.

"Or what?" He laughed again, then ripped the bonnet off my head. "You got beautiful hair, Rachel. Beautiful blonde hair."

"Please give it back."

He only laughed again in response. He touched my hair and my cheek very roughly.

I heard the sound of the bell on the Englisher's door, and my body felt like it was shrinking from the inside. I had hoped to get my bonnet back before my father returned from talking with Mr. Lopez.

He walked around the Englisher holding my bonnet and sat down next to me in the buggy.

"This your dad?" said the Englisher, waving the bonnet in front of us.

I looked to my father, expecting him to answer. He stared ahead, ignoring the Englisher as I should have done.

"You want it back?" he sneered. "You can have it back. Just reach for it. Just grab it from me. Come on."

I began to reach when he pulled it away. "Am I making you angry?"

He was making me angry, and because of that I felt even more ashamed. But I did not answer him.

Eventually, he got tired and he threw the bonnet at me. It landed in my lap. I scooped it up in my hands and was about to affix it when the Englisher leaned in and spat in my face.

I sat there, hot and wet, wanting desperately to do something. But I knew it was not allowed, and that to act on my impulse would risk meidung. I simply put my bonnet back on, disregarding the spittle on my face and the Englisher's string of obscenities.

Once my bonnet was properly affixed, my father started the buggy back home. My heart was still thumping hard in my bosom, my entire body trembling slightly. I didn't understand it. Everything was right again, and I had conducted myself properly. The shame had mostly passed, and the anger, and yet, my skin was still flushed deep red. Yet my body was still in an excited state.

It was a new and indescribable feeling, at once the same and quite different than the shame and anger I felt in the moment. It faded fairly quickly, and as it melted away it seemed to congeal in my belly, a pleasant sleepy feeling.

Over the next several nights, the incident kept repeating itself in my brain. I wish I could say that it happened in my dreams, that I had no control over it, but that would be lying. I was fully awake when I summoned my Englisher again and again, when he stole my white bonnet, when he handled my face so roughly, when he spat at me and called me filthy English names. My skin became flushed again, and the pleasant sleepy feeling returned and intensified with each remembrance, settling lower and lower, deeper and deeper within me. I felt consumed by it. I craved the feeling. I began to think about the episode even during the day, in front of others who were none the wiser. But it was only during the night that I could let the feeling boil over inside me, only between the sheets of my bed that I could ever be sated.

But even as my rapture intensified with each evening, so too did my feelings of shame. And, in truth, one fed the other: the deeper my shame and the more my feelings confused me, the more wondrous it felt, thus deepening that very same shame and confusion. I began to wonder if I was sick, if a part of me was missing, if I wasn't working properly. And that frightened me; I didn't want to be shunned.

For two whole days I was able to stop by threatening myself with meidung: they're going to find out, this is wrong, they're going to find out and then no one will talk with you, no one will break bread with you, no one will marry you. They will spit at you and call you names loud enough so that you can hear them. They will not look you in the eye and you'll deserve it.

But that did not prove a deterrent. In fact, it was quite the opposite: it made me feel so hideously wanton, and that made me feel better than ever before: I was exhausted by my passion, laid to waste by my climaxes.

After that night, I knew two things. One, that I couldn't stop by myself. That I needed help, help from someone I could trust.

And two: that I didn't want to stop. I wanted-- and needed-- more.

I turned to Leah for help because I felt I could trust her. Others might run and tell an elder; I did not think the reality of it would prove nearly as ravishing, nor did I want to risk finding out. Leah proved a good and loyal friend in that respect; she did not tell the elders.

She was walking with Luke: his hat was dented, her bonnet was black. I asked if I could speak with her privately after her walk.

"I've just finished now," she said, more to Luke than to me. For his part, he seemed disappointed. But he tipped his hat to us and was on his way.

"Luke?" I said.

"He can court me all he likes," said Leah. "It doesn't mean I'll say yes."

"You shouldn't encourage him," I said.

"Well, I'm not going to discourage him." Her eyes darted about conspiratorially. "Or any of the others."

"How many others?"

She seemed to relish the question, but not enough to provide a clear answer. "I like being courted. I think I shall like it much more than being married. Once I say yes to one of them, they'll grow a beard. All scratchy and bristles. And in the interim, stubble, which is even worse."

"I think I would like a husband with a great scratchy beard scraping across my skin," I said.

"Not me," said Leah. "I'd much rather kiss a soft clean face."

"You'd do well not to kiss Luke, black bonnet or not," I said. "He'll tell an elder for sure."

"Well, just because I want to kiss someone doesn't mean I'll do it," said Leah. "I've not turned simple."

As we walked and talked a bit more, it became harder for me to want to broach the subject. I felt as if I only could have done so at the beginning of our conversation, and that I had ruined my chance by asking about Luke. In fact, I now hoped to continue talking about inconsequential matters until it was time to part ways. But Leah didn't allow it.

"So, was there something you wanted to talk to me about?" she asked.

I was at once relieved and greatly agitated that she had asked, and I could feel both emotions inside me, as if one filled up my left and one my right, and as they twisted into each other I found myself paralyzed and stammering. And, just as suddenly, I could move and speak again, and everything came pouring out of me.

Leah listened. She didn't ask any questions, or try to leap ahead by putting words into my mouth. She just stared at me and listened and she smiled at me several times, each smile bigger and more blatant than the one before it. The smiles unnerved me. By the time I had finished the easier part of the story to tell-- recapitulating the episode with the Englisher-- Leah's smiles had congealed into one smile the same way milk from different cows will churn together into the same tub of butter. Still faced with the far more difficult task of relating my actual problem, I decided that her strange reaction to my story-in-progress afforded me a perfect place to pause and reconsider.

"Why are you smiling?" I asked. "He was a horrid man, and what he did was horrid."

"I'm not disputing that," said Leah.

"Then why were you smiling?" I said.

"Because you were," said Leah. "You've been smiling all along. Your cheeks are deep red."

"It's from embarrassment," I said defensively.

"Embarrassed at what?" said Leah. "At having your bonnet stolen? Or talking about it?"

"A little of both, perhaps," I said. I decided in that instant not to tell her about my problem after all.

"Or are you embarrassed because you liked it?"

And in that instant I decided to tell her everything. In a furious whisper, I described the progression of my nightly ritual. I was breathless, and so was she. I imagine that my skin was flushed red, but it could not have been as red as hers. Her mouth hung open, her nose quivered with each intake of breath. And then, suddenly, before I could even finish my tale, she reached out and grabbed my bonnet roughly from my head.

I reached for it, and she laughed, deep and throaty, as she slowly backed away and then broke into a run. I ran after her, my hair whipping about my face.

Leah ran into her father's barn. I followed, cautiously. It was empty save for the two of us.

"Do you like it?" she teased, holding the bonnet up between two of her dainty fingers, jingling it noiselessly in the air.

"No," I said. "Because I know you're going to give it back."

"Mmm," she said. "I might."

I stepped closer, reaching for the bonnet. She swiped it behind her back. "Turn around," she said. "Turn around and I'll give it back to you."

I turned my back to her.

"Give me your hands," she said.

I put my hands behind my back. She touched my wrists with her bare hand, rubbing them gently.

"Hold still," said Leah, the words soft and dry in her mouth.

And suddenly, I felt it: like a cord being wrapped around my wrists. I began to struggle.

"Hold still," she said again. She tied my bonnet into a double knot around my wrists. I made a half-hearted attempt to budge it, but could not.

"Untie me," I said.

"You wanted your bonnet back," said Leah as she moved in front of me. "I gave it back."

"This is stupid," I said. "I know you're going to untie me. You know you're going to untie me. So just untie me."

"You think you know a lot, don't you?" she said mischievously. "You know exactly what I'm going to do and what I'm not going to do, right?"

I didn't know how to answer that. "Just untie me before someone comes into the barn."

"How would we explain that, I wonder?" asked Leah.

"You took my bonnet, and you tied my wrists with it," I said.

"Perfectly innocent," said Leah.

"Perfectly."

"We'd both be blameless," she said.

"Yes."

"That's not very exciting, is it?"

"No," I said. "It's not."

Suddenly, her fingers were upon the top-most hook of my dress. With a deft movement, she pulled it apart, exposing the bare flesh of my neck.

"What a pretty throat," she said. She touched it with her fingertips. My breathing became heavy.

She undid another hook. "Leah, don't."

And another. I felt my insides boiling, hot and creamy. "Don't stop," I said.

And she didn't. Slowly, unrelentingly, she undid each hook and latch with a measured indifference. But she was not indifferent. I could tell the way her eyes burned in their sockets.

She ran her fingers down the narrow line of skin between each unfastened hook and latch. I trembled as her touch moved lower. I bit my lower lip, hard and lovely, as her fingers grew nearer to the low sweet boil in my loins.

"Do you like it?" she asked.

I had to take a greedy breath through my mouth before I could answer. "Yes."

"How would we explain this, I wonder?" she mused. "What if someone caught us?"

The thought pulsed in my hips.

"What if an elder came in?" said Leah. "What if I left you here in the barn, with your hands tied behind your back and your blouse open? What would become of you?"

"I'd be shunned," I said breathlessly. It made my thighs throb.

"You sound as if you'd like that," said Leah maliciously. "You hussy."

Again something burned deep and hard and low inside of me, a pulse spreading inside me like I had a second heart within my abdomen. "Do it again," I said, begging.

"Do what again?"

"Call me a-- a-- a hussy! Call me names."

"You really are a hussy, aren't you?"

"Yes!"

"I want to hear you say it!" Leah demanded.

"I'm a hussy," I said. "I'm a wanton hussy!"

She grabbed me roughly by the cheeks, pulling me to her, pressing her soft mouth against my mouth. I yielded to her instantly, and though being still bound I could not grab her face in kind, I did kiss her back with equal fervor. I could tell from the way her entire lovely body was trembling that she, too, was being consumed by a delicious passion. Our bodies rocked and seized up and were spent and sated. We crumpled up, sweating and huffing for breath.

Leah looked at me, and I at her, and she kissed me gently on my mouth. She fastened my hooks, one by one, before unbinding my hands. She held my wrists tenderly and kissed them, worshipped them, and then she reverently tied my bonnet on my head.

The next night, I invited her to supper with my father's permission. Leah said grace, beautiful words formed by beautiful lips.

We never talk much at our table, father and I, not even when mother was still with us. But the presence of a guest provides an occasion for light conversation.

Father notes Leah's black bonnet, and inquires as to whom her suitors are. Leah names three or four young men, careful to add that none of them have really convinced her one way or the other.

"It is good to be cautious," he advised. "Marry as friends. The love will come after. It's no good the other way. One should be moderate in their passions."

We nodded dutifully. The conversation turned (somehow; I don't quite recall) to my cousin Becky. I think Leah mentioned her.

My father grew very short very quick. "It is not right to even speak of her," he said.

"I mean no imprudence," said Leah. "I just was wondering what it was that she did."

My father bristled all the more. "It does not matter what she did. All that matters is that she did it." He turned to me. "You haven't been talking to--her?"

"No, father."

He turned to Leah. "I would be careful also. Your Christian sympathy might be misconstrued. You do not want to share her fate?"

Leah shook her head, and the dinner table fell silent once more for the duration of the meal. Such is the power of meidung.

Using the pretense of bible study, my father allowed us to sit alone in my bedroom. We weren't lying exactly; as soon as we had shut the door behind us, Leah was reading to me from the Song of Songs: "Your lips are like scarlet thread. Your mouth is lovely."

And then she kissed me, sweet and dizzying. It was nice, pleasant, as if we were a man and his wife gently fulfilling the duty of our bed.

But it was also empty, bereft of that deep low feeling inside me, that feeling that I craved, that I needed to be alive.

"We must be careful," she said between kisses and caresses. "If anyone caught us, we would both be shunned."

And there, like a magic key twisting its way into me, that wonderful feeling I craved suddenly blossomed like a faint glimmer of dawn. It quickly began to fade, and, wanting to hold onto it and stoke it to a bright shining broil, I pulled her ear close to my mouth and begged her to say it again.

"We would be shunned," said Leah.

"They'd spit at us," I said.

"They might," said Leah. Then she drew back, wrenching up her face and spitting in mine.

"Do it again," I begged.

She did it again, taking her time as she gathered the saliva within her hot mouth. It splashed right on my nose, exploding sticky and wet on my cheeks and running down into my mouth. "Oh!" I cried out.

"Ssh," she said quietly, at once deadly serious and stoking the molten ball in my belly. "You want your father to catch us? You want him to take us to the elders?"

"Then they'd all spit on us," I said breathlessly. "And they'd scold us, they'd call us filthy names! Yell at me, Leah. Call me names!"

"I can't yell at you," said Leah. The flat lines of her lips suddenly crooked at the corners: "You Jezebel."

"Keep going," I whispered, panting. "Call me a whore."

"You want to be shunned, don't you?" said Leah. "You want everyone to know what a wicked girl you really are."

"Oh, yes," I said. "They need to know. I need to be shunned. I deserve it."

"You're getting too loud again," said Leah nervously. "Give me your bonnet."

I quickly handed it over. She shoved it in my mouth.

"Not a sound," said Leah.

I nodded fervently. My entire body had surrendered to that second heart-beat deep within my ache, every inch of me pulsing with each shrill breath I sucked in through my nostrils.

"Now this is for your own good," Leah said. She spat on me a third time, and it was like water hitting the hot surface of a griddle. I bit down on my bonnet as I felt my body start to rock towards its next climax.

"You need to be punished," she added softly. Then she slapped me across the face. Hard on one cheek, then the other. My head whirled with each blow, my cheeks stung red and tears blistered from my eyes. I bit down harder on my bonnet as I was once more consumed.

Afterwards, Leah kissed my flushed cheeks sweetly; they crackled tenderly.

"Do you love me, Rachel?" she asked. "Or do you love what I do to you?"

"I love both," I said.

"That's not an answer," she said.

I told her that I loved her.

Over that summer, our little games increased both in frequency and extremity. It became normal for her to gag me with my bonnet and to beat my rump red with a nice hard stick. The things she said were more obscene with each occurrence, as if she had to top what had come before. She tied me up with ropes, each one being more difficult to extradite me from; she removed more and more of my clothes: each incident increased the possibility of being caught and the probability of being shunned, and so each incident increased the sublimity of my passion. It became all I thought about, all I wanted, and at my beckoning, Leah fed the fire within me by choosing more and more dangerous places to have our furtive meetings.

This reached its apex that night in August, a night that is as memorable as that evening so many weeks before when my bonnet was first stolen.

I had for the last several nights been begging Leah to do it to me in the center of the village, where everyone could see. Obviously, I was being facetious, but just as obviously, I was not. I became obsessed by the idea, and as we held each other lovingly afterwards she asked if I wanted to do it for real.

"In the middle of the night," said Leah. "When everyone's asleep."

The idea made me flush all over again. "Someone could still see us."

"In the moonlight?" said Leah. "They wouldn't know who we are. They'd probably just watch us," she said, nibbling on my ear. "Watch the unrepentant hussy bending over the well completely naked as she's soundly thrashed on the ass. Staring at your body, listening for your quiet little squeals..."

"Please!" I begged. "Please do it to me."

"Tomorrow night," she said. "Meet me at the well, at half past two in the morning. Completely naked."

"Completely?"

"You're not allowed to bring any clothing," said Leah with a devious flash in her eyes. "You'll have to run and sneak home naked. Wait. I changed my mind." She kissed me sweetly. "You can bring your bonnet."

And I did it. The next night, after I made sure my father was asleep, I stripped off all my clothing save my bonnet, fastened around my chin. I thought about Leah, and how pleased she would be to see me, and how she would reward my obedience.

It was dark that night; the moon had waned to a sliver. I could hardly see, but it appeared that the village was deserted. I could not even see Leah as I bent myself over and braced myself against the well.

I briefly wondered if Leah wasn't going to show at all, and it occurred to me at that moment that this was by far the stupidest thing I had ever done. The potential consequences of my actions were awesome in their inconvertibleness. If I was caught, I would be shunned without any doubt.

It frightened me out of my mind. It also made my body churn.

Every logical part of my brain was spurring me to run. But my body would not listen; it had surrendered to that uncontrollable, ungodly thing within me.

And then I heard Leah's voice. "Take off your bonnet, lover."

I took it off and stuffed it inside my mouth without her even having to tell me. She rubbed her clothed body against my naked one, her covered loins resting against my bottom. She grabbed my hair and pulled it hard. (She knew I loved it when she pulled my hair.)

Suddenly, she stopped. "Ssh," she said, even though I hadn't said anything.

There was silence, and then the sound of footsteps.

"Someone's coming," she said. "Run! Run!"

The instant she said it, my body was dancing with the most intense pleasure I have ever felt. We're caught, we're caught!, I thought. I let out a lusty scream, my bonnet falling from my mouth and lilting down into the well.

I did not have any time to recover; Leah had already started running and I could tell that the new footsteps were getting closer. I broke out into a run, huffing and panting, running not towards my own home but in the perpendicular direction, rushing into the darkness.

When I was content that I had put enough distance between me and my pursuers, I walked home. I walked quickly, but I did not run, as the sound might draw attention.

I slipped into my bed, but I did not sleep. I was worried about Leah, but more than that I mourned the loss of the precious bonnet that had started it all.

We were never caught. And, indeed, no one in the village ever said anything about the two mysterious girls at the well. But things were also never the same again.

Our close call had soured Leah on such adventures. Our games became less frequent and far less dangerous. She hit me only half-heartedly, made sure we were both completely clothed and unbound, and any insults she whispered were mild in case they might be overheard. At the slightest sound, she would stop and check if it was safe.

And though we are still good friends to this day, we are no more than that. The promise of her black bonnet was soon fulfilled, and her husband soon grew a beard. We shared our last and most beautiful kiss two nights after her wedding.

The next summer, I too wore a black bonnet and I too was married.

I love my husband, and will bear him a third child before the year is through.

But I've never felt anything with him like I did that August night with Leah and the well. And I haven't really told him about those days. I don't think he'd understand.

He refuses to spank me or spit on me. He will not call me names or bind me or pull my hair. My husband shudders at the very thought of meidung and will not even joke about it.

He does love me.

But he does not love me enough to be cruel.

DONALD

The last time I tried to kill myself, Angie stopped me.

There are two ways to hang a man. One is to break the neck. Fix the rope to something sturdy, put him on a chair, kick the chair away, and bam: neck's broken. Painless and quick.

But that wouldn't work for me. There was nothing in the apartment to fix a rope to, other than maybe the shower rod, which I didn't think would support my weight.

The second way is to strangle him. Wrap the rope around something, hold it in your hand, and pull. It's far more painful, can take a long time, and if you're doing it to yourself, you can stop it any time you want. You have to really hate yourself to do it this way.

The thing I remember is the tightness around my neck, a tightness that seemed to spread to my whole body. As it became harder to breathe, I felt small tingles of numbness in my body and especially in my brain. I wondered if I was going to pass out, and if in doing so I would release my grasp of the cord, rendering the whole venture for naught.

Angie started calling for me. I pulled tighter and harder. Maybe I could finish it before she found me. But no such luck.

She unwrapped the cord frantically, tears streaming down her eyes. She kept shouting, "Why are you doing this?" Over and over again.

I didn't answer at first. I was a little dazed, my brain still fizzing from oxygen depravation.

"I don't want to live," I said finally. "I want to be dead."

But that wasn't a good enough reason for her. She kept staring at my neck, where the cord had dug into it and made a welt. "Your neck," she said. "Your beautiful neck." And this too was repeated, like a mantra.

Angie made me promise never to do it again. I always keep my promises.

It took a few weeks for the welt to disappear. It upset Angie to see it. I started wearing my four turtleneck sweaters in rotation, using the Monday-Thursday rule to get as much mileage out of them as I could. (Whatever you wear on Monday you can also wear that Thursday without washing it.)

This hid my neck pretty well, but when I was changing or when I went to bed, she still caught sight of it. She would stare at it; sometimes she would touch it; she would say very quietly, "Your neck. Your beautiful neck."

Once she asked me how I could do this to myself, and to her. "Don't you know that I love you?" she said. "Don't you know how much losing you would hurt me?"

I didn't want to hurt her. I told her not to worry. I had made a promise, and I was going to keep it.

I don't want to say that I necessarily have a desire to be dead. I like being alive, and so in that respect I was lying to Angie when she asked me why I tried killing myself.

It's not a desire. It's a drive. It's an urge. This maddening feeling, this oppressive and suffocating feeling, an overwhelming amount of pain and I just want it to stop. I ask God over and over again to take it away. That I'm not strong enough. That I can't take it anymore.

Sometimes I feel like he's listening. Like things are going to get better, just around the corner. If I can just hang on just a little bit longer, it'll all turn around.

It feels that way for Angie too. She said that when she met me, her luck had finally changed. That now our luck was going to change. Any day now. Any month. Always darkest before the dawn.

"What if you give up, and the next day was going to be when it all was going to change? We're that close. I can feel it..."

But it's like Zeno's Paradox. No matter how far I move forward, it seems like we can never reach our destination.

And it discourages her too. I can tell. She doesn't hide it very well. She doesn't hide anything very well. Angie's completely without guile. I wish I was. I wish I could be a whole lot more like Angie. Wish I could be a good person.

I wish I could be honest. Tell her exactly how I'm feeling, exactly what I'm thinking. Sometimes I do, and I almost always regret it. I don't want to hurt her, I don't want her to worry.

I don't want to be dead. I really don't. But when I get twigged out, I have this urge to run down to the laundry room and glug down the bleach. I imagine it burning my throat as it seizes my heart, squeezes it hard, sending hard ripples and painful spasms through my body. I worry that it would make me throw up before it killed me, and that Angie would find me and call an ambulance and save me again.

I also remind myself that I made her a promise, and that I have to keep it. I wish I thought of that first, but I don't.

Sometimes I'm not even that down and I think about it. When I'm cutting vegetables, I imagine plunging the knife into my belly and pulling it across, allowing my intestines to spill out. I think about holding them as I fall to my knees. I wonder what they feel like in my hands, how heavy they will be, how slimy, what texture.

When Angie and I go for a walk, I always give her the wall. That way, if I want to leap in front of an onrushing car, she has less of a chance of stopping me. My body twitches when I see a suitable candidate. Part of me says, go, go, go! But my body never does anything more than twitch.

She suggested that I see a doctor. "You won't talk to me," she said. "Maybe we can find someone you can talk to."

"I talk to you," I said.

"Not really," said Angie. "You go around for days or weeks being moody, and I ask what's wrong, and you tell me it's nothing, that you're fine. And then I find out that you're not fine. And if you'd just tell me right away, maybe you wouldn't spend all that time carrying it around."

This was true. But when she said stuff like that, it didn't make me want to tell her about it. It actually had the opposite effect: I have to do a better job keeping it in. I can't break down and tell her, because that just hurts her and I don't want to hurt her.

Of course, trying to hold it in more just makes it build up worse and worse until it spills out again. And then she worries even more, and the whole cycle starts anew.

I hate to see her worry. It consumes her completely. I used to have trouble getting her to come because the whole time she couldn't stop obsessing about the bills or work or her health. She couldn't enjoy herself. When she worries, she's absolutely incapable of enjoying herself.

And, in turn, that means I can't enjoy myself. I can't be happy when she's unhappy. She's everything to me. She's the only thing that's keeping me alive.

When we first started dating, I wouldn't let her get unhappy. I was aggressively cheerful; it never let up. It helped that I used to be funny. I used to have jokes and stories, dozens of them, and as soon as she had started laughing at one, I launched into another.

The problem with the pace I was keeping was that I eventually ran out of material. I had told her all my jokes more than once. She got tired of my stories. The new ones I came up with didn't have nearly the same sparkle. I used to be funny. I used to make her laugh.

I wish I could again, especially now, especially when she needs it. She doesn't sleep much anymore. She stays up most of the night, staring in the dark, unable to let go of her worrying. I know she's worrying about me. I know that I'm hurting her. Her worrying-- my depression-- it's killing her, it's slicing her up.

She doesn't smile very much anymore. I'll ask her what's wrong. Ask her how her day was.

"It was fine," she'll say. "I'm just a little blue."

"Any reason why?"

"No reason."

"Something I did?"

"No."

"You just worrying about stuff?"

"Not really." And she wasn't lying. I could always tell whether or not she was lying. "Not really thinking about much of anything. My head's just empty. I don't feel like doing much of anything anymore..."

I try to make her happy. I try to make her laugh. Usually she just nods kinda dumbly, like she only half heard me.

We try to go to movies that won't depress her. Movies with happy endings, where the dorky guy gets the girl, or the cool guy stops the terrorists, or the whacky sidekick makes anachronistic wise-cracks and pop culture references in a fairy-tale setting. I'm not a big fan of those movies, and it's hard to disguise my dislike of them.

"Well, I liked it," Angie will say. Then we'd get into an argument woven not so much from yelling and screaming but an uneasy silence.

Sometimes I do better than others about keeping my mouth shut. Then I'll get, "Thank you for sitting through it with me. I know you didn't like it. I just can't take anything that's going to bring me down."

It's hard to see her this way. Harder, because I know it's my fault. I did this to her. Before she met me, she would laugh and smile. She would cry. Now she doesn't even do that. It's like she has no emotions left at all.

"I feel weird," she said. "I don't feel like me anymore. I don't feel like I'm even alive."

"Just hang on," I said. "We're in this together. We'll get through this. Things are going to change, and soon, and for the better."

But she believes it even less than I do. I just keep bringing her down.

Even if things do change-- if I get a better job, or we win the lottery-- I don't think it would make that much of a difference. I would still be depressed, and she would still worry. It's who I am and it's who she is, and a little luck isn't going to change that.

I know that if she left me, I could never survive it. I love her and that's all that's keeping me alive.

But if I died, I think she would still be okay. She's strong like that, much stronger than I am. I need her to live, but she doesn't need me. She worries, but she would be okay. She would move on. Probably find someone who deserves her, someone who can actually take care of her.

Maybe it's her luck that's supposed to change. Maybe I'm holding her back.

And the thought of that, coupled with the way she's being whittled down, makes me so angry at myself, it fills me up with self-hatred. I think about jumping off a building, or setting myself on fire, or tying a bag around my head. I think about starting the car and setting it in reverse, letting it roll down the driveway. I put my head down on the pavement, and the wheel rolls over me, breaking my nose with a splurt of blood before squashing me painlessly dead and flat.

But I don't do it.

For now, I love her more than I hate myself.

It's not always sad. I know there are happy times even now. She has smiled and laughed more than once in the last week or so. I did enjoy myself, we did have a good meal, we did go for a good walk. But I have to remind myself, and worse, I have to remind her.

Depression has a way of obscuring the good things in your life. It focuses you so much on this moment, and on itself, that it's like you've never had a good time ever in your life. And even when you remember it, even when you find a specific example to counter the charge, it feels so far away, so out of reach, that it just makes things worse. You can remember the event, but not the feeling.

I keep telling myself that I can't take it much longer. That I've just about reached my breaking point. But then I keep going.

I would welcome a break-down. Something that dramatic would shake things up. Whether for good or for ill, it would be over. Finally, at long last, the pain would be gone. But I never quite get to that point. It just gets worse to worse, but I never hit bottom. I just keep falling.

Deeper and deeper. It never ends.

It never will end.

No end and no relief. I'm not allowed. I made Angie a promise, and I'm going to keep it.

TUCK

We finalized the divorce this morning. Cordelia got the money and the house; I got the cat. We had lunch together after and I agreed to pick it up in a couple of days, after I had time to get things settled with the apartment.

"I'm glad it's ending like this," I said. "It was painful but this is kinda amicable. Kinda friendly. It wasn't bitter. If it had to end, I'm glad it ended like this."

"It didn't have to end, Tuck," she said. "Don't act like you had no control over this." She pointed at me accusingly with her fork. "You did this, Tuck. You chose this."

"I didn't choose this. I didn't say, hey, maybe I'll make her divorce me."

She rolled her eyes. "But you knew. You knew what would happen."

The waitress came by and topped off our water. I caught her staring at my boobs again; her eyes quickly flitted to the fresh stubble on my chin before averting my gaze completely.

Cordie waited until after the waitress had left before picking up right where she left off. It was a knack that she has; she had whole sentences in her head, and if one was interrupted she would remember it precisely. I think she did a lot of practicing in her head, a lot of rehearsing and editing, because a lot of what she said always had a kind of flowery quality to it. And this was one of those times.

She said, "You're not getting SRS, you're doing heart surgery. You cut out my heart when you did this, and it hurts. It hurts so bad. Or it did. I dunno. It doesn't hurt so much anymore. It's over now."

"We can be friends after my change, can't we?" I said. "We can hang out, right?"

"No," said Cordie. "I don't think we can."

I'm on a month-by-month with the apartment. It's a bit pricier than I'd like, but I don't plan on staying a real long time. In two months I should get the go-ahead for the really major surgeries: most (but not all) of my penis will be removed: the head will be reshaped into a clitoris and the skin inverted for my vaginoplasty. After that, I've got some minor cosmetic surgeries (mostly facial restructuring) and a lifetime of hormones and then (viola!) I'm a woman.

It'll be a new life, and a new apartment. I really want to start over. Wherever I go, I'll be a woman. If I stay in this apartment building, I'll always be the freak, the in-betweener. I'll always be alone, one person in two bodies.

I found a box of her stuff when I was unpacking. I'm not sure how it got there. I guess it was left over from when we had moved into the house. So many of those boxes never got unpacked.

I spent a few minutes looking through it. I can't say it was a box of memories or anything like that-- at least, not our memories. Mostly stuff belonging to her parents, and they were dead long before we found each other. She talked about them sometimes, but mostly I think she wanted to forget about them. That's probably why she never found the time to open it.

I set the box aside and turned to unloading my own boxes. Strangely, they don't feel like my own. There's no memories in them, no resonance—just things, objects, clothes. It's like they don't belong to a person at all.

I guess it comes with being all uprooted. In a state of transition and all that. It made me feel vaguely inhuman, and that put this weird little idea in my head, and I said to myself, the next box I open, there's going to be a memory in it. You're going to open it and you're going to see or touch something and it's going to remind you of something, it's going to remind you of thirty-five years on this Earth and counting.

But there's nothing. The boxes are full, but they feel empty.

It took a little while, but I convinced myself that this was actually a good sign, a sign of progress. That I was already closer to my new life than the old one. That I wasn't Tuck any longer.

I still haven't chosen a new name, though. I've flipped through some baby-naming books now and then, but I hadn't really made a concentrated effort since Cordelia filed for divorce.

But before that, we thought that maybe we could make it work. Mind you, she wasn't exactly happy about me wanting to become a woman. But she was willing to talk about it with me. "We've got each other, we're equals, we said we'd be honest with each other and so let's be honest. Let's be adults and let's talk this over."

And we did, over the course of several nights and weeks. We talked about the medical procedures, the psychological rigmarole, about our marriage, about happiness, and about names.

"I'm so used to calling you Tuck," she said. "I don't know if I can get used to calling you anything else."

"Well, you'll have to," I said. "If I get it done." (I was still very much waffling back-and-forth on the matter at this time.)

"What name do you want?"

I didn't know. "But something very feminine, very pretty."

We looked up some names online. Rachel means lovely; Elise, a diminutive of Elizabeth, means God's promise.

"Apparently," she said, "Leah means tired and weary. You have to admit, that's very feminine."

We went to the library together to get some baby-naming books. We took them to the girl at the check-out desk, and she immediately started beaming at us. "How long?"

"How long what?" asked Cordie.

"You don't look very far along," said the girl. "For your baby."

"I'm not pregnant."

The girl apologized. "Are you, uh, writers then? Picking names for characters?"

"Yeah," said Cordie. "Something like that."

"I don't want you to get mad at me, Tuck. But I want to say something to you."

"Sure, anything."

"We had talked about children, remember? When we got married?"

"Yeah..."

"We kept putting it off. Money, et cetera.

"But.

"I'm not getting any younger, Tuck. I'm. I'm not going to have any children. Am I?"

"You would have been a great mother, pookie."

She started to cry, which was rare for her. But even her tears were orderly: composed.

"I would have been a terrible father," I said.

"You don't even want to be a husband anymore," she said.

"I'm still... I'd still be your partner. I'd still be the same. Just the gender would change. But on the inside, I'd still be Tuck. Whatever name we pick for me."

"But I won't be the same," said Cordie. "I'd be different. I'd never be a mother, and I'd stopped being a wife. I'd be a dyke. I don't... I don't even know how I'd feel about that..."

"You don't really enjoy it as it is," I said. "Maybe after, it'd be better for you..."

"I don't want a woman," said Cordie. "I really don't. If I wanted a woman, I'd have chose a woman. I want a man. I love a man."

"You love me."

"Yes. Yes, I do. Though sometimes I wonder why..."

"You love me, and that's for keeps, right? Better or worse, et cetera? Look, Cordie. Cordelia. Baby. If I was in an accident, if I lost half my body, if I couldn't walk..."

"God, don't say that..."

"You'd still love me, right? You married a man who could walk, but if I couldn't, you'd still love me?"

"Yes."

"Because I'm still the same inside," I said. "Only the outside changes. Don't you see? I won't be turning into a woman. I've always been one, all along. You've been in love with a woman all this time. A hairy, smelly, ugly woman-- true. But a woman. Baby, please. It's not worth it if it's not with you."

Like I said, we tried to make it work. I went through about a year of psychological evaluations and prep work and all that fun stuff before I got my boobs. Cordie had been back-and-forth about the whole thing up until that point, and I think it was after I brought the girls home-- after it had started to become real-- that she decisively made up her mind.

"I can't do this," she said. "I can't deal with these, these things. I know they mean a lot to you. I know that this means a lot to you. But I really can't do it anymore. Please. If you love me. Go back and have them undo it."

I told her I'd think about it, that I needed some time. She conceded me that much-- she never wanted to be the kind of person to force an ultimatum on me.

But more time didn't help the situation. Seeing my gorgeous breasts juxtaposed with my hairy belly only strengthened my desire to become fully female. And the longer I kept them, the more frayed things became between the two of us. Long arguments punctuated by longer periods of silence. We sat in separate rooms and slept on different floors.

I went back to work shortly after my operation, and shortly after that, I was fired-- basically, I think, because of the operation, though my lawyer's still trying to prove that.

Cordie believed it, though. But she wasn't on my side. "Don't you see how ridiculous this is? Is it really worth losing your job?"

"If they're going to treat people like that, it's not really a job worth having, is it?"

"What about your wife?" And there, in four little precise and polished words, there was the ultimatum that had been lurking all these long months.

She filed for divorce the next week.

I brought the box by this morning. She stood in the doorway in her bathrobe, opening the screen door just enough to accept the box. She pulled it over the threshold.

I watched her open it through the mesh on the door. She smiled weakly.

"Thank you, Tuck."

"I chose a name," I said. "Gemelle."

"That was my mother's name."

"I know. Is that alright?"

"Sure."

"You don't mind?"

"No." She smirked somewhat smugly. "You'll probably change your mind again anyway."

"I think I'll keep that one. It's nice. Very pretty."

"It means 'twin'," said Cordie.

I just kinda nodded.

"Are you going to take Pacino with you?"

"Uh, not today," I said. "I was thinking, in a couple weeks I'm going in for, y'know, the operation. I'm going to be in the hospital and stuff, and you said you'd take care of him while I'm gone, right?"

"Hmm-mm."

"Well, I was thinking, that might be a little stressful for such a little guy, shuttling back and forth. So why not just wait until everything's settled, and then when he moves over, he moves over, y'know?"

"That's fine," she said. "I can hold onto him for a little bit longer. Don't make it too long, okay? He doesn't really like Joey all that much." Joey is her boyfriend.

"He doesn't like anyone," I said, giving Pacino a scratch behind the ears.

"No," said Cordie. "Just his daddy."

GEM

I lost my virginity for the second time in the men's room of a bar. It doesn't really matter which bar, and it doesn't really matter who the man was, either; I was a little drunk and in a rush to take my new body for a spin, so to speak. It was... it was. I mean, I could certainly feel something moving inside of me, pulsing and warm through the condom. But it wasn't pleasurable and it wasn't painful. It just was.

I didn't think I'd have an orgasm right off the bat. I know that it's harder for a woman than a man. But I had sort of built up this anticipation in my head, I had wondered for so long how it would feel—I had imagined it, tasted it, felt it with my brain for so many months-- and so I expected there to be, y'know, something. But there wasn't.

And, y'know, that's fine. It was never really about sex anyway. But it was still very disappointing, another in a long series of disappointments.

I had a few boyfriends, and then a few girlfriends, but nobody-- not even the legendary Joanne de Cloots, championship clit-licker of three counties—could untangle my tingle. I tried everything-- from vanilla to kink and back again-- but with no results.

When I look at myself naked in the mirror, I want to see a woman. I want to see Gem. But bits and pieces and chunks of Tuck are still there, still poking through: the shape of my thighs, the stockiness of my torso, the bones in my face. Even after a few more operations-- cheekbones heightened, chin smoothed, nose narrowed-- the beautiful smooth face I wanted is beyond my reach.

Some days, it's all too clear that I will never really be a woman, that all I've succeeded in doing is making myself an in-betweener-- half-finished, never to be whole again. On those days, I want to take it back so badly.

But that's just the thing. I can't take it back. I'm stuck with what I've done, and what I've lost-- everything I've lost-- I've lost for good.

At least that's the way it seemed for five long lonely years. Sure, I dated, I cohabitated. But I also hated, hated myself very deeply. I tried to take my life many times.

And it didn't used to be that way. I was never my biggest fan, but all this anger, all this self-loathing-- it was a new thing, like it had been grafted onto me with the new parts, like it was shot into my veins along with the hormones.

Before all this happened-- when I was Tuck, when I had Cordelia-- I was happy. Or at least that's what I tell myself now. The pain I've got now is closer to me than the pain I had then, so it's easy to minimize it. But, when I'm honest with myself, I remember.

I remember being unable to move and unable to think. I remember wanting so desperately to be happy and so desperately wanting to be anyone but me. I remember trying to tell Cordie. It wasn't that there weren't any words. I had words, mountains of them, powerful words, but when I spoke them they lost their power, they dwindled to grains of sand-- gritty and inelegant and completely incapable of expressing whatever it was that was inside me. I remember trying to show her, trying to make her understand how big a deal it was-- and I know that I wasn't happy then.

I remember the long months before I told her, before she even knew I had been into her clothing, how much I wanted to tell her and how afraid I was that she would leave me.

And she did leave. She divorced me, and the last time she saw Tuck was when he dropped off a box of her parents' stuff a couple of weeks before the big operations. I was supposed to take Pacino home after the change.

But I never came back.

Five years after my life started over, I saw her again. She had aged the five years and then some, all packed underneath her eyes. I recognized her instantly.

I wanted to talk to her; I didn't know what I wanted to talk about. Part nostalgia, part curiosity, a lot of love and tenderness and pain. I wanted to apologize, and I wanted her to apologize to me all at the same time. It was very much like the pain in the old days, wanting to tell her but being afraid, wanting to speak things that were ineffable.

Ineffable. Now, that's a Cordelia word. I always said that she had poetry in her, and that Tuck had none. I think I have a little now. Five years will do that to you, I guess.

But I just kinda stood there, in the grocery store, staring at her, watching her, falling in love with her all over again. I didn't say anything, didn't try to get her attention.

As she turned away from the bell peppers, though, she looked at me and saw me staring at her. She didn't stare back-- just kinda shook her head and muttered. Then she turned away and went back to her shopping.

She didn't recognize me. Didn't know who I was.

I wondered for a moment if I had made the mistake: there had been times in the past when I mistook passers-by for my ex-wife.

But it was her.

I wanted to do something. Had to do something. But I didn't know what. And so I let her walk out of my life again.

That night, I went over my life again and again. I didn't sleep a wink, and I kept at it through the morning.

I arrived at the conclusion that I made a gigantic, colossal mistake when I got my sex changed; shortly thereafter, I arrived at the conclusion that it was something that I had to do. That I had no choice. I couldn't live as Tuck.

But I couldn't live without Cordie, either.

All-in-all, I was feeling pretty low. And just when you thought it couldn't get any better...

I lost my job that day. Like so many jobs before it, somehow someone found out about the operation. That's not the reason they put down on paper, of course, and every single time they'll deny it up and down in court and, every single time, they've won.

But the fact is, no one wants a freak. No one.

I decided to go to the library. I wouldn't exactly call it a quiet place-- too many kids running around for that-- but I still found it calming. I like reading, and a decent book would give me something else to focus on. That was my thought, at least.

As I muddled and puttered on through the rush hour, I got kinda emotional. I started crying; my mascara ran down my cheeks in big black blobs. And I prayed. For the first time in a long time. For the first time in this lifetime.

I prayed to God, and I said something along the lines of, I know You're not supposed to give us more than we can carry, but I don't think I can carry much more than I've got. That I was breaking down. That I was broken and tired.

If we all have a purpose in life, then I felt like I didn't have a purpose, or that my purpose was to be a joke and to suffer. "I want something good in my life." I said that a few times: I want something good in my life. I want to be happy.

And I got to the library, and I parked my car, and I cleaned up my make-up. And I said to Him, "It'd be nice if I could see Cordie again. It'd be nice if I went into the library and there she was. I'd really like that."

And I walked into the library, and there she was, sitting in a chair with a stack of books on her lap, one of them cracked open and absorbing her attention. I sat in a chair perpendicular to hers, without the pretext of a book or a paper, and she looked up.

"I know you," she said. "You're the woman from the grocery store. You were staring at me yesterday."

"I'm sorry about that," I said. My voice cracked.

"Do I know you? Have we met before?"

I shrugged.

"Well, why were you staring at me?"

That was very much like her; she hadn't changed much at all. And there was something about that, about the edge in her voice and the bluntness with which she conducted herself, that I had found very appealing the first time we met. Something sad and sweet swelled up inside me. "You're very beautiful."

"Are you trying to pick me up or something?"

"I dunno," I said.

"I'm not--"

"No, you wouldn't be."

"I'm very flattered but--"

"I didn't think you were. I'm sorry. I don't know what I'm doing."

"Did you follow me here?"

"No."

"It just seems odd, that you'd show up twice in a row and stare at me."

"I was just coming here just to come here," I said. "Helps me calm down when I'm feeling blue. But I..."

"But you what?"

"Never mind."

Cordie closed her book around her index finger. "Do you really want me to never mind, or are you just saying never mind so that I can drag whatever it is out of you?"

"I was hoping you'd be here," I said. "I had no reason to think you would be. But I prayed in the car, on the way, and I prayed that you'd be here."

"So you could talk to me?"

"I guess. I dunno. Again, I'm sorry. I know this was weird. It was nice just talking to you, though..." I started to get up. Part of me would hope that she would stop me.

She didn't.

About a week later, I'm walking down the street with my groceries when she honks her horn at me.

I approached the driver's side as she rolled down her window.

"Well, well, well," she said. "If it isn't my stalker." She smiled. It had been a long time since I had seen that smile. "This time I know for sure if was an accident. Unless you were praying?"

"No," I said.

"Where's your car?"

"In the shop."

"How far do you have to go?"

"Just a couple of blocks," I said, nodding towards the apartment complex where I had moved in about three months before.

"Well, that's not far at all."

"Nope."

"Well, be seeing you." She started to roll up the window. I motioned for her to stop. She did, though she didn't roll the window back down. "Yes...?"

But of course, I had nothing to say. So I just shrugged and stared down into my groceries. She sighed, rolled up her window, and drove off.

She did a Uie and parked across the street. She got out of the car. "So, what is it that you want from me?"

"I don't know."

"I'm not a dyke."

"I know. You said that already."

"You don't even know me."

"I'm crazy, okay?" I said. "I'm just crazy."

"You're not crazy," she said. "You're sad. And you're alone. And I understand that. I'm sad, and I'm alone. But I can't be with you, okay?"

"That's fine," I said. "I know that. I'm not usually crazy like this. Usually, I'm okay. Just—I dunno, I get around you and I get all mixed up and it's weird."

"This ever happen before?"

"No, never."

"Not with anybody?"

"No."

She stared at me for a long time. "Well, obviously fate keeps throwing us together, and who am I to fight it? Maybe we're supposed to be friends, and maybe we're supposed to be bitter enemies, but either way, we've got to stop meeting like this. So. My name is Cordelia. And yours?"

"Gem."

"Short for something?"

I swallowed. "Gemelle."

She blinked. "That's my mother's name."

I figured then that the whole thing would be up and out in the open. But it wasn't. I thought for sure she'd have to remember that I had chosen her mother's name. She didn't seem to have any inkling who I really was, or rather, who I had been.

It's weird; I look at myself and all I see is Tuck poking through, jutting out like a bunch of knives. But there was this one girlfriend who was surprised when I told her that I was a transwoman. She said that I looked very feminine. I thought she was lying to me, trying to be nice to me.

But here was Cordie-- and a sharper pair of eyes I'd never known-- and she had no idea that I was her ex-husband.

We started hanging out, started talking. The connection we had had before, that uncommon rapport, had started up all over again. Like a second chance. Though this time it was strictly platonic.

But it wasn't all sunshine and peaches. The fact was, I was lying to her. She might not have known it, but I did.

Part of me was worried that she would find out; part of me was worried that she wouldn't. It was just like the old days all over again. Wanting to say something, hating myself because I couldn't, but being paralyzed by the fear.

And part of me knew that I was falling in love with her all over again. I couldn't stop thinking about her, I couldn't stop wanting her. But I knew that this new relationship was founded on it remaining just a friendship. If I made another pass at her, if I tried to make it anything more, she might just cut me off completely.

And so here I was, yet again: crumpled up with pain because I wanted to tell her I loved her, and just as crumpled up because I knew that if I did I would lose her again. Each alternative more terrible than the other, each moment I spent in her company more excruciating than the last.

Two or three months of this, and she invited me over to her apartment for the first time, confident, I guess, that I wasn't some nutjob who was going to strangle her at a moment's notice.

"Oh, shit," she said. "You're not allergic to cats, are you?"

"No," I said. "I love cats. Do you have one?"

"Yeah," she said, opening the door. "But he's not very friendly. Only person he liked was my first husband."

For all our talk, we never really dived into the past. Whenever anything like that came up, I was pretty scant when it came to details; I think because I was guarded, she didn't feel the need to reveal much herself.

She offered me some tea and I said yes; then I asked how many times she had been married.

"Twice," she said.

She briefly told me the story of myself, leaving out the entire transsexual thing.

"So, what happened?" I said.

"He died," she said.

"Oh," I said. "I'm sorry to hear that."

"Yeah, well... what can you do?" she said. "It was a pretty bad time. I still miss him a lot."

"He... he sounds like he was a pretty special guy. What about your second?"

"That was about a year later," she said. "I rushed into it. I think part of it was, Tuck didn't really want to have children. He made that abundantly clear." She rubbed her cheek with the flat of her hand. "And I'm not getting any younger, you know? So I wanted to have kids, and here was a guy who wanted them. But he... he wasn't the right guy. Wasn't much of a husband and he wouldn't have been much of a father."

"So you never had any?"

"No," she said. "First couple years, and nothing. We went to a doctor. Turns out I can't have a child." She threw up her hands. "Joseph left me after that. Found someone nice and young and fertile."

"I'm sorry," I said. "I didn't ask to upset you."

"That's okay," she said. "So. What about you? You ever been married?"

"Um..."

"I'm sorry," she said. "I forgot."

"Well, I wasn't always a lesbian," I said. "I had a few boyfriends. Sex wasn't great. Hell, it's not great with women either. Truth is, I haven't had an orgasm in over five years."

I could tell this line of conversation unnerved her.

"You ever been in love?" she asked me.

"Once," I said. "Once, almost a whole 'nother lifetime ago. But I let her go."

"Why?"

"I don't know," I said. "I made a choice, and that choice cut her out of my life. But at the same time, it wasn't like I really had a choice. There was something inside me. I mean, it was my fault. It was totally my fault, and if I could take it back, I would. But at the same time-- if I had the choice to do-over again, I don't know how I could have done it differently. Because the thing inside me was eating me up. I was in a lot of pain inside, and if I didn't make the choice I did-- I'm just gibbering on. I'm sorry."

"No, you're not," she said. "I understand. I totally understand what you're talking about. But here's the thing, Gem.

"Whether you would take it back or do it over differently or whatever, that's irrelevant. I learned that a long time ago.

"There are things I wish I did different, but wishing doesn't make it so."

"I don't know," I said. "I prayed and there you were."

She smiled at me. "You're sweet. You really are. You're a good friend, Gem."

And so we drank our tea, and we talked of other things, things that weren't of any importance and thus the most important things we could talk about.

And then, after about the third cup of tea, I became aware of the fact that she was staring at me. That's when I looked down in my lap and noticed that Pacino had curled up there, and that I had been scratching his head and his fat little belly. He never let anyone do that-- except for his daddy.

I looked back up and into Cordie's eyes, and I saw the hurt there. And then she called me by a name I hadn't answered to in five long years.

"Tuck."

I nodded. "Back from the dead."

ELISE

I never had much interest in sex, growing up. I wasn't a late bloomer, per se; by the time I was sixteen I had all the necessary parts in place and ready to go. And I certainly took an interest in the opposite sex, and they in me. I had dates, I fooled around, and I lost my virginity, all at pretty much the same time as all my friends did. But I didn't feel anything. Sure, I could feel them poking around in there, and I could feel their hands on me, but I didn't really enjoy it. There were no sparks, no fireworks. There was something wrong with me.

All the women's magazines provided guides to inducing a better orgasm, but I couldn't even have one to begin with. I'd even settle for a bad one. And I'm not just talking about during sex. I couldn't even bring myself to climax. I masturbated a lot, but still nothing.

At the time (this was my teens and through my early twenties) I invested a lot of importance in this. But at a certain point, it became apparent that it just was never going to happen, and by thinking so much about it and worrying so much about it I wasn't doing myself any good. I was feeling really inadequate, incomplete, and for what? I never had that strong of a libido anyway. I didn't need to be bringing myself down like that.

So I just stopped caring about it, and just got on with my life, and you know what? It worked. I didn't feel empty or incomplete without an orgasm. Sex isn't the most important part of a relationship. Love is.

I heard about people who break up because of "sexual incompatibility", and I thought, Jesus, what's wrong with these people? Someone won't suck your dick good enough and so you leave her, abandon your kids, something you've spent years building together? What a crock of shit! It's like leaving someone because they overcooked a chicken. That's not love. That's people acting like children. So petty and so stupid.

Of course, knowing what I know now, I can see why it would be that important for some people. I mean, I still stand behind my basic assertion here-- that kind of attitude is frankly ridiculous and immature—but at least I understand where they're coming from. Back then, I didn't. Like I said, I didn't really care about sex, in or out of a relationship. All that mattered was love.

And that's what Patrick and I had, right from the start. I mean, it wasn't love at first sight or anything. He was such a dork and a screw-up sometimes that I basically just settled for him. But he fell so hard for me, idolized me so much, and he tried so hard to make me happy that I realized what a great guy he was. (Is.)

So it took a while for me to realize that I loved him. But the more I look back on it, the more I can see that I didn't settle for him. I chose him, just as much as he chose me. I was always comfortable around him, I could always be honest: the love had always been there, it was just waiting for me to notice it.

I told Patrick things I had never told anyone before. I let him know upfront that while I was happy to be intimate with him, that I didn't particularly enjoy it. He took it as kind of a challenge. He tried all sorts of different ways to turn my crank, but he just couldn't seem to get me revved up. He was never too annoying about it, and he never made me feel like it was my fault I couldn't come. (Though a lot of the time I did feel that way just the same.) Other times, when he was too discouraged to put too much effort into it but still horny, he humped me quickly so it wouldn't take too big a chunk out of my day.

We dated for several months, then he proposed. I said yes and we eloped a couple of weeks after. There wasn't any real progress on the sexual front for our first year together, but like I said it didn't really matter much. We enjoyed each other's company, watched movies, played scrabble, argued, reconciled. One month gently folded into the next and we settled into a pleasant, mellow, matrimonial rhythm.

That all changed, quite abruptly, the day I had my first orgasm. I was in my dentist's office, getting a cavity filled.

The worst part about the dentist is the procaine needle. It's not so much the prickling or stabbing sensation as it is the feeling of the needle sliding through the roof of my mouth, moving into my head. The hygienist removed the needle and the upper right side of my mouth started to go numb. It's not gradual like the gas, slowly spreading into the lungs and out into the body, but a very sudden change like shifting gears on a truck: my mouth slammed into Numb abrupt and heavy.

You know what? I take that back. The worst part is the dentist. It's not the physical pain (see above) or the thought of him scraping away at my teeth, but the humiliating process of being told how bad my teeth are. Have you been brushing?, yes, I've been brushing, twice a day?, yes, twice a day, and flossing? regularly?, yes. Well, I don't understand it then-- just keep breathing deeply-- because these teeth are in terrible condition. I'm sorry. Don't say you're sorry to me-- say it to your teeth they're the only set you get and they don't get better they'll only get worse so you better take care of them if you want to keep them, yes? Yes.

The dentist grabbed some toweling and swabbed at my mouth, which was no doubt geysering probably my entire blood supply. The thought made me shudder, and I closed my eyes so I wouldn't see it. The inquisition was over also. The void left by his stern chattering falsetto was filled with music. Bach I think. And it was glorious.

It flooded over me, seeped into me with every breath of the gas, invaded me, reprogrammed me so that my body lived to the music. Occasionally I'd hear the evocative and mysterious whine of the drill, accompanied by a vague pressure against the heavy numbness in my mouth. But mostly-- my eyes closed, my body prickling beautifully-- I was living in a world of sound.

I lost all sense of time or thought, aware only at the edges of my consciousness that there were other people in the room, that they were moving about me in someway I couldn't define. The music stirred something deep and primal in me, and by the time the radio switched to Bruckner-- I'm positive it was Bruckner, seventh symphony, scherzo-- I was coming loud and hard.

As soon as it was over-- and it was over much too quickly-- I became acutely aware of the white light blistering against my closed eyelids. I opened my eyes and saw my dentist and my hygienist staring at me. They asked if I was alright, how many fingers were they holding up, was I in any pain? I reassured them that everything was fine.

"We'll use less gas next time," said the dentist finally before he finished his work.

As soon as we got into the car, I told Patrick. He was hard to read-- he's always hard to read!-- but I guess I would say that he happy for me and resentful at the same time. And I understand that much, he had wanted to be the one to finally make me come for the first time.

He tried to make light of it. "I try for a couple of years, and nothing; Bruckner does it first time, right out of the gate, and he's been dead for a hundred years."

But by the time we got home, though, he was pretty excited about it. We started fooling around. He was probably feeling friskier than I was, and he was real eager to get me off. "Twenty-eight years on this earth, Elise, and you've only had one orgasm. We've got a lot of catching up to do."

He put on some music, and I closed my eyes and laid back as he ate me out. Nothing. Just like before. Patrick became despondent. I had to talk him into going inside me. He didn't take long, and he came, and we cuddled. Both of us were pretty disappointed. We tried it again the next night with the same depressing results.

But, I looked at it this way: I've had one now, so I know I can do it. It's not hopeless. At the same time, I had this new thing bugging me, which was: what if Patrick can't make me come? Isn't that going to make him feel worse? Hell, what does that say about me?

I kinda wished I hadn't had it at all, or that at least I hadn't told him about it.

Two months passed and nothing happened. We tried Bruckner and Beethoven, Mahler and the Gershwins. We even tried roleplaying, in case it was the environment that did it for me: sometimes, Patrick took the role of the dentist and sometimes that of his buxom assistant.

But nothing happened.

I guess I shouldn't have worried about Patrick because he took it in stride, like he always did. But it was still frustrating in its own right. I was starting to wonder if I was ever going to have one again.

You know, there's that saying-- that it's better to have loved and lost than never to have loved at all-- but that's bullshit. Nostalgia's a bitch. I'd rather have never came than done it just the once, like some kind of freak accident that could never be repeated. Now that I knew what I was missing, it was driving me crazy.

I wanted to come again, I wanted it probably more then than Patrick ever did. I tried masturbating again, but to no avail: it got me wet and made my clit a little sore, but no bada-boom.

And, frankly, it really pissed me off. Sure, I never really cared about it before and, sure, there were and still are more important things in my life. But there are women who talk about having these multiple chain-reaction orgasms and look forward to having sex and they actually enjoy it. So why not me? Why did God (or whoever) have to make me different?

The feelings of inadequacy just kept piling up on top of me. Over time, I started to let it go again. But a couple of weeks before my next dentist's appointment I started to get my hopes up.

The day arrived. There was music, there was gas, and there was procaine: I complained of feeling pain and so they bumped the gas up to the same level as last time. I felt numb, sure, and I closed my eyes, and the music got into me-- but there was nothing. Not a spark, not even a sprinkle.

I drove myself home, rejoining the snowstorm already in progress. (I had needed the car to run an errand for work before the dentist, and so Patrick got a ride with Joe.) My mouth felt heavy and still quite numb, and I'm sure I was drooling by the gallons.

I had been looking forward to it, I had actually wanted to go to the dentist, and for what? Nothing.

I was feeling like maybe it was a freak accident after all, that first and only time. I was feeling pretty low, and I was feeling silly for feeling low over something that I kept telling myself was so trivial, and that, of course, made me feel even lower.

By the time I got home, it was dark. (One thing I hate about winter: the early sunsets.) I pulled into the driveway. The porch light refused to blink on (supposed to have a motion sensor). Great. Just great.

I fumbled with my key and the lock for several long seconds, trying to stab it into the golden slit and being just a little off this way or that. I unlocked both locks and opened the door.

The house was pitch black too. Not a single light was on. I flipped the switch near the door. Nothing. I called for Patrick, asked if the power was out. (Another thing I hate about winter.) There was no answer. I called a couple more times-- still no answer-- before taking a few tentative steps forward.

I wasn't scared exactly. The power does occasionally go out. The house was securely locked. I'm a big girl, and I can take care of myself. Patrick may not have heard me, or he might still be out with Joe after work. I called him again. He didn't answer. That's when I heard the heavy creak of the floor.

It was sudden and loud, and of course I hadn't been expecting it, so I wasn't quite sure what direction it had came from. I stood very quietly, listening for another sound. Nothing.

I got out my cell phone and opened it up. The faint blue light hardly lit up the two or three inches in front of it, but that was better than nothing. I wanded it back and forth as I stepped forward through our rather hazardously-kept living room, making my way towards the electric torch on the top of the entertainment center.

I didn't see it up there, and my whole body tensed up very suddenly. I felt a nervous tingling in my abdomen, a very palpable sense of anxiety. Thirty seconds having passed, the light on my cell phone blipped off: the strange anxious feeling ratcheted up considerably, like someone was inside me, twisting a screw that made everything tighten and contract—like my body was one huge lung expelling a breath of air.

I pressed a button on my cell phone to make the light blip back on. My muscles expanded, taking in new air.

Then I heard it: someone rushing towards me from behind. I whirled around and he grabbed me, laughing maniacally in my face, his teeth bared. I dropped the phone and I came, soft and lovely, as I realized it was Patrick who now held me in his arms, the torch lighting up his features from below. He mistook my gasp and immediately began launching into his usual apologies.

"Shut up," I said, and I kissed him.

"The power went out," he said. "I was just trying to surprise you, not really scare you. I guess I should have," etc.

"Shut up," I said again. I undid my pants and slid down all four layers-- jeans, leggings, panties and socks-- all in one swoop. "Turn out that torch."

And, well, to make a long story short, Patrick knows that when a lady takes off her pants and tells you to turn out the torch, you shouldn't ask any questions.

He said afterwards that it was nicer than usual-- that I was more "carnal"-- and he asked if anything happened at the dentist. And so I told him more or less what I've just recounted.

But I didn't feel nearly as positive about it as I did the first time. Sure, having it happen a second time buoyed my spirits a bit. But when I actually stopped to think about it, I didn't feel any closer to being normal. When Patrick went inside me, nothing had changed: it still felt vaguely like someone picking my nose.

(Patrick just looked over my shoulder at what I just wrote and said there were boogers coming out of my twat. Lovely. He's so mature.)

It would be different if it was a sex thing, a physical thing. The body would react differently to the different sensations and that might trigger an orgasm. But both times there was no actual sex involved, which made me think that they were related somehow, that there was something the music at the dentist's office and the darkened living room had in common.

And so I found myself faced with a mystery, and since I was never any damn good with mysteries, it was very disquieting.

It was at this point that Patrick took the initiative to consult an expert-- or, more properly, a sexpert. He wrote to a columnist in one of the alternative weeklies, explained the circumstances behind my two orgasms and the epic failures of the past.

The sexpert suggested I was turned on by feelings of helplessness and vulnerability, that we should try some light bondage and D/s, see if that did the trick.

To make a very long and embarrassing story short, we did try it, and the sexpert was very, very wrong. Patrick was as uncomfortable being anything but incredibly accommodating as I was playing some bimbo in distress. When the (ahem) toy store refused to accept our returns, I suggested somewhat crossly that we send the sexpert the bill. We ended up selling most of it on craigslist. Everything but the blindfold.

I don't know what it was about it that made me keep it. I told Patrick we could use it in case one of us had a surprise for the other, though really one of his father's old wide neckties would have done just as well. Either way, we held onto it, and near the end of winter, as we were going through the motions of fooling around in various states of undress, I suddenly surprised both of us by asking him to use it on me.

As he put the blindfold over my eyes, I felt my entire body swell with naked anticipation. He tied it fairly tightly at the back before unclasping my bra. I heard a soft schlump as it fell, presumably on top of the rest of my clothes.

Patrick took me by the hand and led me carefully down the stairs. "What are you doing?" I asked. There was no answer. I heard the door sqrueak and he had me stand in the hallway. His footsteps receded away from me.

There was silence for awhile. A chill washed over me.

"What's the temperature set at?" I asked.

"Are you cold?"

"A little nippy."

"Well, I'll turn it up."

"What's it at?"

He only made a soft, humming laugh in response. More footsteps. A few seconds later, the familiar and reassuring sound of the furnace kicking on. Something soft and hairy brushed between my ankles. The cat, on his way to vent-bathe.

Suddenly, a lot of sounds: creaking floorboards, rapidly moving footsteps, thuds and schlatoks, rurks and thurps. I tried to place them: furniture being dragged over carpet, being moved, things displaced? I figured that's what it was, but I couldn't figure out what was being moved and where. I tried to sketch it in my brain, but there were too many sounds, too much movement. It made me slightly dizzy and confused. And that made me more-than-slightly wet.

"Come on in," said Patrick.

I stretched my arms out before me. I felt for the entertainment center and it wasn't there. My hips bucked enthusiastically, like there was a fist centered deep inside me, punching outwards.

I walked further into the room, meeting no resistance, no objects. I knew they had to be somewhere, knew that I could bump into them at any time. Each step I took that revealed nothing was another step towards something, and so it provided no relief. My body became quite warm and flushed.

Suddenly, I heard a sound that I recognized: the window blind. "Did you just put up the blind?"

"Maybe," said Patrick.

I heard another sound. "Did you just put it down?"

"Maybe I did," said Patrick. "Of course, that's only one blind accounted for," he added evilly. "Maybe I put one up while you were in the hallway. Oh, there's Mrs. Denver outside our window. Hi, Mrs. Denver!"

Now, I'm not an exhibitionist, and I don't get off on being exposed or humiliated. So the thought of someone being outside didn't turn me on in the slightest. But the fact that I didn't know one way or the other-- that, being deprived of my sight, I had no way of knowing, that, perhaps, I would never know-- well, suffice to say, that did it for me, big time.

And that was it, that was what had been turning me on all along: not being aware of my surroundings, being deprived of one of my senses (such as sight) and solely dependent on those remaining.

Why? I have no idea. I don't buy that Freud bullshit that it originated as a result of some childhood trauma or some other nonsense. But whatever the reason, all I knew was that it worked, and over the course of the next few weeks (and years, actually) it yielded proven results.

One orgasm followed another as we tried different variations on the same theme. We added earmuffs to the blindfold, making me wholly dependent on touch and taste. I had no way of knowing when Patrick would touch me, or how he would touch me, or where. More than once, I got myself whipped up into such a frenzy that I could have sworn there were two sets of hands, or three, exploring my body, two mouths, two lovers, an orgy that was really just Patrick after all.

But that was only during foreplay. I didn't really feel anything during the actual intercourse, and Patrick knew that. I wish it was different. We tried to find ways to combine the two, the sex and my orgasm, but they seemed to occupy two completely different spheres.

Patrick's libido seemed to dwindle after those initial weeks following our discovery. He was more than happy to play these little games with me, to make me come, but he more often than not didn't want to come himself. Sometimes when I asked him to help me get off, he seemed a bit reticent. I could tell he was starting to resent me, and that, of course, was making me resent him. The long and short of it was, I stopped asking, instead waiting for him to offer.

And, don't get me wrong-- he did offer. And we did have intercourse. It wasn't like everything suddenly stopped. But the resentment was growing softly inside us.

And that was scary. That was very scary. Like I was saying before, I have no sympathy for people who let their relationships go to pot because of sexual incompatibility. And I didn't want that to happen to us. Partially because it was so ridiculous and, more importantly, I loved Patrick so much that I didn't want to lose him.

I started praying a lot, very desperately, and I told God that Patrick meant more to me than any damn orgasm. If the things required to make me come made Patrick feel small, I'd rather not come at all. "It's okay if I never come again," I said. "Just please don't take Patrick away from me."

But, as it turns out, I was able to keep both. And there was no miracle involved, not unless you count a birthday as a miracle. It was my twenty-ninth.

Patrick had me put on the blindfold, and he led me to the car. I asked where we were going.

"I've been doing a lot of thinking," he said. "The most important thing in the world to me is to make you happy." He talked awhile then about all the times before when he had tried to give me an orgasm. It wasn't so much that he wanted to feel virile, he said, but that he wanted me to be happy, as happy as I made him.

I interrupted him, said that he did make me happy before, that this wasn't important.

"It isn't but it is," he said. He wanted to make me happy in all ways, just like I made him happy in all ways. It was kind of gushy, but at the time it touched me very deeply.

"And now you can have an orgasm," said Patrick, "and that's great. But I'm not the one that gave it to you. And before you even start, it wasn't the dentist, either. It was you. You don't really need me."

"That's not true," I said.

"Sure, I was there, and I helped, but at the same time, it's like I don't count. You don't come with your body, Elise, you come with your head. It's all you, baby. Not me. Well, that's the way I felt, anyway. And maybe I still do feel that way a little bit. But it comes down to this, Elise.

"I love you. And I want you to be happy. And so maybe I can't make you come when we're making love, but you know what? I can still help out in some small way."

"In a big way."

"So," he said, "however it happens, whatever kind of sex you could call it, I want you to enjoy yourself sexually. I'm sorry I've been kinda sore about it."

I still didn't understand where this was going, but Patrick refused to answer until he brought the car to a stop. He told me I could take off the blindfold. We had been driving for about an hour.

"JCU?" I said. "Why are you taking me to college for my birthday?"

"They've got a sensory deprivation tank," said Patrick. "I've paid to give you a session. And so either this is just going to be weird and trippy and a really stupid present, or I'm going to give you the best orgasm in your life."

I tried to describe it to him afterwards, and even now when I try to describe it I find that I simply don't have the words. I'm no good with abstracts. Details I can handle-- but what details can you recount when you can't feel, can't see, can't hear, can't taste, can't smell, can't taste? Inside the tank, you can't even think. It was like I was completely cut off from my body, from the world, surrounded only by the vast ocean of myself.

It was the strongest, best, purest orgasm I ever had. I don't know if it lasted the entire hour or just five minutes. And even now, at thirty-two, having gone back five times in the interim, none of those that followed, incredible as they were, have ever touched the first.

Once I got out of the tank, I got dressed and found Patrick waiting for me in the lobby. "You're glowing," he said, and he smiled; I think at that moment that he was even happier than I was.

After that, our sex life returned to what passes for normal. We play our little games and we make love, and we cuddle afterwards, usually until Patrick falls asleep, snoring while my head rests on his shoulder.

LEON

Stacy's birthday was the occasion of our first argument. We had agreed ahead of time that until our financial situation improved we would not buy gifts: a simple card would do. Stacy was very adamant about this, and I had no reason not to take her at her word.

About an hour before she came home from work, I scurried through my collection of birthday cards until I found one my grandmother had given me four years before. I crossed out my grandmother's name and signed my own before altering the text of the card to read "to a special girlfriend" instead of "a special grandson".

I left the card on the dining room table, the dining room being adjacent to the apartment door. I turned out the lights and lit a few of the scented candles that Stacy had always shown a preference for. I inserted one of her favourite compact discs into the player, an anthology of love songs that had often served as a preamble to our couplings. In short, I thought I had did everything correctly and that she would be satisfied.

She was far from it. She pretended to cry when she saw the card, and she pretended to get angry when I asked her what was amiss.

"You said you only wanted a card," I said.

"A card from you," said Stacy. "Not your grandmother."

"But it is from me," I corrected, pointing out that I had changed the salient details. "I don't understand why you're upset."

"It's the thought that counts," she said. "And you just weren't thinking!"

Looking back at it now, I of course can reach the logical conclusion: she had wanted a present. She used the ridiculous pretense of the card to mask the fact that she had wanted a present without appearing to want one.

My friends had told me how beautiful Stacy was before I met her. I found her to be highly symmetrical, large-breasted, and in possession of clean, healthy skin, all very much in keeping with prevailing standards of beauty. The group I was with laughed many times at several of her comments, and she generally held the attention of persons of both genders: every conversation orbited around her, she was often asked to recount apparently amusing anecdotes from her life, and most of the group's decisions were made at her suggestion or whim.

"She's a lot of fun," one of my friends said after. "A little crazy, maybe, but she's a lot of fun." Most agreed with this sentiment, stating that while she was often flighty and undependable, they derived great pleasure from her company.

These qualities made her a very good candidate for a girlfriend. I added her to the three or four others on my mental list of possible girlfriends, and weighing the pros and cons of each one over the course of the next several weeks, I found that Stacy was creeping steadily towards the top of the list.

The only real negative, her flakiness, was actually a positive as well because that ensured the relationship would not overstay its welcome. I figured it would take roughly two weeks of courting to win her over, and that our relationship would last about four to six months after that, which would allow us enough time to celebrate my birthday while still cutting it short before

Christmas and the expenses that it entails.

With time thus being of the essence, I quickly contacted her and told her that I was attracted to her. I pretended to stutter and pretended to look away, and she pretended to be touched by all this. She said that she was attracted to me, too-- that she could tell that I was a serious and passionate man: I seldom laughed, she pointed out, and my eyes were always observing everything with a "terrible intensity". Stacy was like that, prone to exact and dramatic word choices that she probably thought would sound profound.

The truth is, I didn't laugh because jokes are still the one thing that throw me. All the rest of it, I've got pretty much down pat. I know to smile when something fortunate has taken place. I know to cry when someone has died, and to let my mouth hang open when I first get the news. I know that when I am supposed to be angry, which happens very infrequently, I am required to tense up my muscles, flare my nostrils, kick inanimate objects and mutter expletives.

And I know that I am supposed to laugh when something humourous has occurred, but that's just the problem: I have no way of knowing when something humourous has occurred. While concrete, definable circumstances surround the other emotions, I can only piece together "funny" from the context clues—if someone else is laughing, for example, or if the person speaking is smiling excessively and speaking quickly. In those cases, I am poised and ready to laugh at a moment's notice. I have to listen carefully to the speaker in order to anticipate the shift in vocal tone that generally accompanies the "punchline".

But it's still extremely inexact. Sometimes someone is smiling simply because they're happy and not because they're telling a joke, and so my laughter is inappropriate. Sometimes, if they are especially bad at telling the joke, the vocal shift occurs before the punchline and I end up laughing before the funny part. Perversely, if someone is considered to be very good at telling a joke, there is no real shift between the set-up and the punchline. In fact, many of the mannerisms I have come to associate with "telling a joke" are not present. In those cases, when others in the group end up laughing hysterically, catching me unawares, I had found it useful to explain my lack of laughter with the words "Very droll".

But after a few embarrassing encounters (generally laughing too hard at what was apparently not a very funny joke), I had decided it best to simply not laugh while still being somewhat sociable. I was alternatively considered "moody", "serious", or lacking in a sense of humour. And I found, much to my surprise, that I was not ostracized for this missing part.

I think it's the only part a human being is allowed to be missing. If you're missing some other part-- happiness, sadness, desire, anger, love-- it can be quite dangerous.

And so I pretend.

I think everyone pretends, and I think my relationship with Stacy really cemented this idea for me. She was always pretending, always the center of attention, always "on". She embellished stories to apparently make them more entertaining. She spoke very loudly and moved without any hesitation or warning, always performing, always making an entrance or an exit or a scene.

She even admitted as much to me once. She said that only around me could she really be herself. That she had to put an act for the rest of the world and she didn't know why.

But she was never really herself around me. She used emotions as an excuse to act illogically and to make unreasonable demands of my attention. She cried often, and she yelled often, for no reason that I could ascertain.

I don't think anyone has any emotions. We're all liars. We've been told that we're supposed to have emotions, that people without them are freaks, and so we lie so that we fit in, avoid that stigma. A lot of people have convinced themselves that they have them after all, and I would feel pity for them if there was such a thing as pity.

Something always had to be wrong with Stacy. She had an appetency for turbulence. Most people, when you ask them what's new, the answer is invariably "not much".

But with Stacy, something was always new and something was always on the brink of disaster. It didn't make any sense; she couldn't just let things be. It was extremely confusing for me.

I tried to point out to her the illogical way in which she was acting. I attempted to use calm, clear reason-- the only thing that separates us from animals and plants-- to make her stop all this crying and screaming and nonsense. But she was impenetrable.

During one particularly bad argument, she started hyperventilating. I could see that this conversation was not going anywhere good anytime soon. There was no point in having it. And I told her that much. I said, "This conversation obviously isn't going to solve the situation. I'm going to see a movie."

And then I left.

And the really bizarre thing was, when I got back, she hadn't calmed down; she pretended to be even angrier with me. In fact, she told all her friends what had happened and they, too, thought I had acted improperly.

Sometimes I think I'm surrounded by morons.

Looking back at our time together, I've come to the conclusion that either there was something wrong with her brain, or that she was extraordinarily and intentionally devious. It wasn't just that she couldn't follow a basic and perfectly logical argument. It was that the basic patterns of the emotion game were skewed.

I know how the game is played: stimulus A demands emotion A, stimulus B emotion B, and so on. Winning the lottery demands ecstatic happiness, generally demonstrated by jumping up and down, pumping one's fists into the air, and screaming joyously at an intolerably high decibel level. Whereas winning tickets to a sporting event or concert on the radio requires the winner to say "Really?" in a very surprised voice, followed by meaningless ebulliences like "Oh, wow" and "Cool". Each stimulus has its own, finely-keyed emotion to be faked. And with Stacy, I was often penalized for coming up with the correct emotion.

Let me give you an example. Conveniently, two different conversations only a few days apart neatly paralleled each other. On the first occasion, I was penalized for making a mistake; on the second, for getting it right.

During the first conversation, Stacy was recounting the story of the time she crashed her car about a year before. My previous experience with car wreck stories was that one was to respond with shock and concern. And so I did.

"Oh my God," I said. "Are you okay?"

And she looked at me like I was an idiot, and I suppose in that instance I was: I had overreacted. I realized that if the accident had happened more recently, then that reaction would be the proper one; because it had happened a year before, the situation required a more subdued response.

I didn't want to repeat the same mistake, and, when a few days later, she told me about the time five years before when she was raped, I gave the proper response. "Oh, that's too bad, then."

And then, inexplicably, she acted as if she was enraged and we got into the biggest row we had had up to that time. It was insane.

And so, either the wires were crossed in her brain, in which case she thought anger was the proper reaction to my reaction, or she knew exactly what she was doing and was maliciously trying to drive me out of my mind.

As time wore on, I began to suspect her more and more of the latter. That's probably why during the last month or so of our relationship I embarked onto a bold new experiment.

During one of our arguments, she said something along the lines of, "Why won't you be honest with me? I just want you to be honest with me. Just be yourself."

Now, most of my previous girlfriends had said something to that effect, and it had never really phased me before. But this time, I thought, why not? Why not drop my safety net, why not stop pretending?

Maybe, I figured, maybe that's what she really wanted. Maybe she realizes that emotions are a big giant fraud, and she wants to see if you know. So I called her bluff. I started being myself.

The first thing I noticed in this new stratagem is that it greatly reduced our conversations. I no longer felt it necessary to give lip-service to such domestic trivialities as "That's nice, dear" or "How're you doing?" I stopped inquiring how her day was, as I had no real desire to find out. She persisted in asking me, though, and I answered when I felt like answering.

I stopped saying "I love you", as I knew it wasn't true. Sometimes she would say "I love you" several times in the row, hoping to prod me to respond in kind. If I said anything at all, it was simply "Okay."

I had thought, and had hoped, that this new stratagem would calm her down. It did not. In fact, she became more erratic. I had thought that by being honest, she would stop asking me to be honest. But quite the opposite was true: she accused me more than ever of bottling up my feelings.

I tried to explain to her that I didn't have any feelings, that nobody does, that they don't exist, that there's no such thing as love. But she refused to listen; she clung to her fiction.

Perhaps at that point in time, I should have doubled-back and pretended to have emotions again. But I remained committed to my decided course of action.

About a week before I was scheduled to break up with her, I found her dead in the bathroom. She had most taken several pills, I was to discover later. I made a cursory attempt at reviving her and called 911 more or less immediately. It would look bad otherwise.

The paramedics also failed.

The funeral was held a few days later. I read a poem but did not pretend to cry. I heard whispers that I was still in a state of shock, that it hadn't hit me yet. Everyone knew I loved her, they said; even her friends, in whose eyes she had vilified me, were supportive and nonjudgmental.

I watched her mother pretend to cry and throw herself over the box. I wanted to tell her how stupid she looked, how stupid they all looked, but I opted not to.

There was no real palpable difference to me between the way things ended with Stacy and the way they did with previous girlfriends. Sure, she was dead, but either way the relationship was over and so, really, I was the same either way. One plus is that her mother more-or-less let me keep all of the stuff in the apartment, so there was no acrimonious divvying up.

I didn't really think about her at all much afterwards. Though about seven or eight months later I came across a photograph of her.

I stared at it for a long, long time.

And I think that I may have felt something then. I don't know what it was; it was only there for an instant. If emotions do exist after all, it's quite possible that it was one of those. But as I had nothing to compare it to, there was no way for me to really be sure.

I don't really think about Stacy anymore, but I do think about that moment when I thought I might have felt something. I wonder if it really happened or, if like I suspect is the case with everyone else in the world, I just fooled myself into thinking it did.

HORNY

I think about sex all the time. From just before I hit puberty right up until this minute, I've been thinking about sex more-or-less non-stop. I imagine having sex with every person I meet in every place I've been. During school I would stare off into space and daydream about getting gang-banged right in the middle of class. More than once I'd be snapped out of it by a teacher who had been calling on me half a dozen times. The entire class would stare at me, and I'd wonder if they knew, if the blush of my cheeks gave it away.

Gym class was worse. Climbing into the shower with the other girls, I couldn't help but look at them, stare at them, fantasize about them. A couple of times I wondered if they had caught me staring; no one said anything. I tried to look away, to turn my back to them, but my eyes almost always found their way back to the visual feast. When I had finished the three semesters of gym required to graduate, I stopped taking it; I loved gym and sports, but I just couldn't risk being caught. For the same reason I never tried out for track, though I would have kicked some butt.

It's not fun, being me, being horny all the time, being completely unable to shut it off, to regulate it, to stop thinking about it. I can't talk to a person without wanting to fuck them, without using them to grease my box, without using them. And I don't want to use people. I want to talk to them, and relate to them, as fellow human beings. But I can't. It doesn't matter who they are:

teachers, friends, family, coworkers, customers, enemies, strangers, men or women, old or young. Everyone turns me on, and pretty much everything turns me on-- the kinkier, the better.

Now, all that being said, I am not a promiscuous person. A pervert, yes, but a nympho, no. Despite my perpetual dampness, I didn't lose my virginity until I was nearly twenty years old. And, as you can no doubt imagine, I had a lot pinned on that moment: countless self-induced orgasms would be a mere prelude to its awesomeness, et cetera, et cetera. And (as is often the case) in actuality it was pretty lame.

I mean, I felt *something* in there, poking around, and (post-hymen) it wasn't painful but it wasn't particularly pleasant either. It just was. It was boring, he took way too long, and I just lay there like a dead fish waiting for some fireworks. But my fuse remained unignited.

That didn't change the fact that I was constantly horny, but neither did the fact that I was constantly horny change the fact that actual sex with an actual person was always a let-down.

Maybe (I thought) maybe I'm too kinky. Maybe I've been thinking about getting it on for so long that vanilla just won't do it for me.

Well, to make a interminably long story short, if my first boyfriend had been any more vanilla, he could have been served with a slice of apple pie. Slater, by contrast, was all for trying out some weird shit. We tried bondage, spanking, role-playing, rape fantasies, pegging, even an ill-advised and best-forgotten threesome. And all that gets me excited thinking about it now (yes, even the threesome), and all that got me excited thinking about it before we did it, but when we were actually doing it, it did nothing for me.

Bless his heart, he tried. He tried to get me off and he tried to figure me out, but Slater always failed on both counts. "I don't get it," he said more than once. "You talk about all this freaky stuff and then when we try to do it, you just lay there and then you say you don't enjoy it."

"I don't."

"Well, then, why do you talk about it?" said Slater. "Do you say it just because you think I'll like it?"

"No."

"Because I'm happy just doing it normally."

And that's a word that stuck in my craw: normal. Why on earth couldn't I be normal?

After a while, we stopped trying the kinky stuff. I'd just lay on my back and he'd go to town and we'd cuddle after he was done. That didn't stop my urges, though; it didn't put an end to my never-ending interior monologue of exquisite debauchery.

I'd still want to talk aloud about all manner of weird things, but that got on his nerves. "Do you really want to do that?" he'd say.

"No."

"Then don't talk about it."

All this tension came to a head one night when we were fooling around. He had gotten pretty worked up and I assumed my normal position so he could harpoon me.

"Just a minute," he said. "I gotta go piss first."

This sparked my imagination and I suddenly flung myself on the floor, hugging his knees. "Then piss on me!"

"Seriously...?"

I churned as I thought of his hot piss spraying all over my face and my tits. "Yes! Do it! Use me as your fucking toilet!"

And so he did.

The taste wasn't awful, but the smell, God, the smell! The smell was terrible, it filled up my nostrils and it wouldn't go away. It stunk and it made my skin sticky and slimy-feeling. My insides dried up instantly.

As soon as he was done urinating, he pulled me up and bent me over the bed. He entered me but I was overcome by a feeling of intense nausea. "Stop," I said. "I'm sorry. I can't do this right now. I have to take a shower. I just feel so dirty."

"You asked me to do it," he said as he pulled out.

"I know, I know."

"Jesus Christ! I'm getting so tired of this shit!"

The argument lasted for several minutes. I just wanted to get to the bathroom to wash his stink off of me, and he just kept shouting at me. The smell kept getting worse and worse, intensifying, filling up my brain. My head pounded and wave after wave of revulsion rippled up from my belly. I was afraid that I was going to throw up. It finally got to be too much and I fainted.

When I awoke, the argument resumed, though at a calmer tempo. But our differences had become irreconcilable. I used his shower for the last time, got dressed, and never returned to his apartment.

And while I won't be mentioning him again, I should note that this was not the last time I saw him. That's because this story isn't about me and Slater.

It's about me and his sister.

Vivian was only fourteen when a car accident put her in a wheelchair for the rest of her life. Her spine was damaged. Her legs were useless. She has no feeling at all from her waist down.

Now, that's not all there is to her. She's so much more than that, so much more remarkable than that.

But I didn't know that when I met her. When I met her, she was the fat twenty-something in the wheelchair with all the acne. I made pleasant but inconsequential conversation with the wheelchair over dinner and felt sorry for it afterwards. Mostly, I just ignored her, the way every member of her family did. When I did think about her, it was (surprise, surprise) sexual.

There were two fantasies about Vivian that kept cropping up. The more innocent of the two began with a series of contrivances, of people-running-late and missed phone calls, that resulted in Vivian and I being alone in her parents' house together. She'd have to use the bathroom, and there being no one else to assist her, it would be up to me to wheel her in, lift her up, pull down her pants and settle her on the toilet. Sometimes, just before I sat her down, my hand would lightly brush her crotch just as she began to prematurely urinate, the piss running through my fingers. Even after the disgusting reality of actually being pissed on, the thought of it still churns my butter, as the Amish say.

It's strange that I can ignore reality in times like those, that I can still be turned on by the thought of something even after I've discovered that the actual something doesn't really turn me on. But for even the thought of something to turn me on, it has to be possible, it has to be something that I can do in reality. I can't understand giantess fetishes or people putting on costumes to pretend that they're cartoon characters. I've never been able to successfully fantasize about a celebrity, living or otherwise; in order for it to work, it has to be someone that I actually know and something that can actually happen.

And that's why I was disappointed one evening over dinner when Vivian excused herself to go to the bathroom. She pushed her chair away from the table, wheeled into the bathroom, and shut the door. Two or three minutes later, she came back to the table. She was perfectly capable of using the bathroom without assistance, and I was never able to masturbate to that imaginary event again. I remember at the time actually being fairly cross with her about this.

I ended up falling back more and more on my other big fantasy about Vivian, the one that made me feel scuzzy all over. In this one, I'd sneak into her bedroom while she was sleeping and pull the covers off her. Then I'd start fingering her insensate snatch. She'd awaken, but she'd have no idea what I was doing. Sometimes, I thought about bringing a man along to quietly rape her while she lay there, awake in the dark, completely unaware.

I hated thinking about that. I loved it and I hated it and I hated myself for thinking it.

I've always hated myself.

I see in all my self-loathing and waxing erotic that I've neglected to tell you much else about myself, including one salient fact: I repair computers for a living. It seems awfully technical and nerdy, I know, but it's actually the perfect fit for someone with my sort of problem. You can find out a lot about a person by looking at their porn.

Nine times out of ten, that's what puts the kibosh on someone's hard drive; they go to the wrong site, download the wrong link, and voila!: Trojan (and I'm not talking about condoms).

And so, you can imagine my excitement when, just a couple of days before I broke up with her brother, I learned that Vivian's laptop was in need of my expertise. I salivated at the thought of learning what turned her on, so that I might build a new and significantly less-scuzzy fantasy about her that incorporated some of her own kinks and twirls.

The following night, I powered up her laptop and checked over her hard drive and her history. There was not a spec of porn on the thing, not even a nipple, not even a meaningful glance. The virus that had fucked up her laptop was the result of a bad torrent download; she thought she was getting a copy of "That's

Entertainment".

God, I was pissed off. She got a virus from wanting to see some G-rated singing and dancing? "I'll work on this later," I said aloud to no one in particular. "You don't deserve to have me work on you tonight. 'That's Entertainment'. Seriously."

And then, of course, the next day was the aforementioned urine-related argument that ended my relationship with her brother, and so I was in no hurry to get it done and back to her. Over the next two or three weeks, I could always count on a voice mail message from either Vivian or her brother asking me to please fix the computer. After a while, they stopped asking even for that.

"I just need it back," her voice scratched over the cell phone. "I can find someone else to fix it, I'd just like to have it back."

And I'd feel guilty and say to myself, "This weekend, I'll get her computer done." Or "I'll do it tonight after I'm done watching this movie." But the time would come and it would pass and her stupid all-singing all-dancing laptop would sit there.

That's when I got a phone call from her lawyer. I think it was actually one of her brother's friends (I recognized his voice; I always thought it was very sexy), but the threat of a lawsuit will do wonders for your motivation, let me tell you. A few minutes later, I powered up her computer and got to work on fixing it up. It didn't take long at all.

I called Vivian and let her know that it was done. I made some kind of lame excuse at the time, but we both knew how weak it was.

"When can I get it back?" she said.

I really didn't feel like going over to her parents' house again, but I also didn't feel like prolonging the inevitable. "I'll be right over."

I clicked off the phone and was about to shut down the laptop when I was seized by the urge to give it one more good ol' college try: surely there had to be some porn on there somewhere.

No video files. (Well, none that were porn, anyway.) No suspect sites in her history or cache. No incriminating google searches. Nothing naughty in her e-mail (seriously, people need to come up with stronger passwords). Nothing.

Frustrated, I had one last resort; I selected "search" from the start menu and began searching for naughty words. I started with anatomy and worked my way up to verbs. All of them came up negative until I tried "fuck". The little animated dog yipped happily at having uncovered it in a word document called "Diary".

Well (I thought) this might be promising. I opened it up, hoping for something suitably juicy. I used the "find" function and arrived at the first usage or variant of the word:

I am so fucking worthless. No matter what my parents or my friends tell me. This is a fact. An actual fact of life: I am fucking worthless. It's not because I'm in the chair. Plenty of people in chairs build lives for themselves. But I don't have a life. It's not that I wish I was dead. I feel like I'm dead. I don't feel alive.

I don't care about being in the chair. The chair I can deal with. God dealt me that hand and I'm cool with it. But why do I have to be so fat? I'm fat because I let myself be fat. Why do I have to be so ugly? My fucking face. It's like a tomato took a shit all over it.

I was shocked. I mean, she was never the happy-go-lucky positive-thinking sort, so I kind of expected some sad-sack shit. But the depths of her hatred for herself, the sheer brutality of it: her diary had some teeth. It hurt me just reading it. And, like all things, that turned me on.

But it wasn't a strictly sexual thing. I mean, yeah, reading it got me wet, but I didn't really feel a need or desire to touch myself and, as I continued to read her diary, this time from the beginning, I wasn't looking for anything sexy to file away in my memory for later use. I was reading it because it was in and of itself interesting. Not to use it, not to use her, but to read it: to read her.

The passage I reconstructed above was the tamest. As I read on, page-after-page, rambling paragraph-after-paragraph, it got worse. Far worse. I'll spare you the gory details (mostly out of a concern for her privacy) but I'll share another bit that caught my eye.

Bro. came over with his gf. for dinner. [My name] sat next to me. I could smell his cum on her breath. God, I fucking hate her. I want to break her fucking legs so she'll keep them shut. Maybe after he'll dump her. Then he'll start fucking the next pretty useless bimbo he can find. Stupid pretty vacant slut, always smiling at me. Go ahead and smile, bitch. Why wouldn't you smile? You have nothing to worry about. You don't know anything about pain. About suffering. You're beautiful and skinny and I want to break your fucking spine. You couldn't handle that, you weak little shit. You'd kill yourself. I'd like that.

And that's when she called. "You said you were coming over two hours ago."

I powered down her computer. "Yes, I'm sorry. I got caught up on something. I'll be right there. I'm actually really seriously on my way out the door." As if to provide evidence of this fact, I jingled my keys loudly next to my cell phone.

I got in the car and started driving over. About half-way there, I started to regret my haste. I should have saved a copy of her diary onto my flash drive, I realized. Once I gave her the laptop back, I would never see it again. Never get to read it again. I considered calling her and telling her I forgot to do one more little thing on it but I chickenshitted out before I even finished dialing. One interstate and three turns later, I was at her door. There were no cars in the driveway. Everyone else must have gone somewhere, leaving her there to stew.

I knocked. She answered. I handed the computer over with an apology. She thanked me and she shut the door.

I stood there a moment, wishing I could have done it over, that she had invited me in or that I had manufactured some excuse to enter. When you spend a lot of your time in your own head, you do a lot of mental do-overs, of what-ifs. Sometimes I forget that you can't actually do that in real life.

I went back to my car and just sat there. What was I waiting for? What was I doing? I didn't know. I just didn't want to leave yet. I wanted to talk to her. Connect to her.

But what would I say? The way she slammed the door, the angry way she answered, and especially those words from her diary: she hated me, she wanted to cripple me, wanted me to die. Why on earth would I want to make a connection with her?

But I wanted it just the same. Her words had done something to me. Even if she hated me, that was fine; I hated me too. I hated me more than she did. Probably about as much as she hated herself.

But from what I had read, there was no reason for her to hate herself. She wasn't a pervert. She didn't use people like I did. She didn't think about doing the things to them that I did. She wasn't a bad person. A bitter person, sure. She was bitter and she had things to be bitter about. But no reason to hate herself.

I got out of my car and went back to her door. She answered. "How much is it?"

"What? No, you don't need to pay me. Not after I made you wait like that."

"What do you want?"

"Can I talk to you? Can I come inside?"

She shrugged and let me in. "Do you want some tea?"

"Sure. Do you need any help?"

"No," she said with a snort. "I can do it myself." She wheeled herself into the kitchen and got started.

I followed her, hesitantly. "I..."

"Hmm?"

"Nothing. I just... I..."

"What is it that you want?"

"I want you to know that you're beautiful."

Her upper body shook with a quick jerk of a silent laugh. "Thanks."

"I mean it. You're beautiful. You're a good person."

"Inner beauty," she said dismissively. "Well, I hate to burst your bubble, honey, but not all retards are angels and not all cripples are optimistic."

"I didn't mean it like that," I said. "You're a person. People are complex. You're not perfect but you're not bad either. You're beautiful inside and out."

"Yes," said Vivian, "as you know, I'm quite the debutante."

"I mean it, though," I said. "I really mean it."

"Look, where is this coming from?" she snapped. "You're trying to make me feel good about myself? Well, fuck you. You don't know me, lady. You don't know what it's like to be me. So I don't need your pity."

"I'm not giving you pity."

"I know what I look like," said Vivian. "No matter what you say, you can't change that."

"So what do you look like?" I said. "What's so bad about the way you look?"

"I'm a fucking whale, for starters."

"You're beautiful," I said. "Your body's just different, that's all. I actually think you're pretty sexy."

"I've yet to find anyone else who thinks so. And even if I was skinny, it wouldn't change my face."

"What's wrong with your face?"

"Look at it!" she shrieked. "Look at my fucking face!"

"Your face is beautiful," I said.

She screamed and grabbed the teapot by the handle. She swung her arm towards me and the boiling water splashed on the bare skin of my arms.

"Oh God," she said immediately afterwards. "Oh God, I'm sorry. I'm so sorry."

"It's okay."

I went to the sink and ran them under the water. It burned like crazy at first, and then gradually the cold water made my arms numb.

"I'm so sorry," she said again. "You see, I am a shitty person."

"It's okay, really," I said. "You're not a shitty person. You were just angry."

She seemed to get defensive. "You kept pushing me."

"I wasn't," I said.

"Yes, you were. Please don't start again."

"Vivian." What I had to say was important and I felt like I should say it looking into her eyes. I tried to turn my head towards her but it put too much strain on my neck. And so what I said, I said while staring at the blisters on my arms:

"Let me tell you what I think. I think every person is sexy. I do. I think every man is handsome and every woman is beautiful. They're all just different, that's all. There's nothing ugly. Just different. Just intriguing. Just sexy."

"Pimples aren't sexy," she said.

"Oh, but they are. Look, look at your face. You cover it up with make-up to try and hide your pimples and your acne scars. First thing I'd do-- uh, hypothetically, you know, if I was, if I was-- first thing I'd do is I'd wash off your make-up. Scrub it off your face. And then I'd kiss it. I'd kiss every one of your pimples. Suck them. Lick them. Taste them. Worship them. Do you have acne anywhere else on your body?"

"I have some down my chest."

"On your breasts?"

"Yes..."

"Then I'd, I'd take off your shirt. Leave your bra on first. And I'd put my face in your boobs. I'd kiss all the pimples I could find, I'd try and stick my tongue underneath the bra so that we'd both get a little frustrated, a little hot. Then and only then I'd take off your bra and begin sucking on your breasts, sucking on your pimples, sucking on them long and hard and wet."

"And... and then...?" She cleared her throat.

That's when I realized what I had said, what I had been saying, that I was saying it out loud. I turned towards her, taking my arms out from the water. They began to sting again almost immediately.

"What would you do next?" she said, breathlessly.

"I'm sorry," I said.

"What?"

"I wanted to come here and talk to you. To tell you how beautiful you are. To do something for you. And now I'm... well, I'm using you. I wanted to do something, I wanted to treat you like a person, and instead I'm just using you to make myself wet."

"This is making you wet?"

"Very."

"I think it's making me wet, too," said Vivian. "But I'm not sure." She grabbed one of my wrists, just below the burn. With her other hand she pulled back the waistband of her sweatpants. She slid my hand inside.

I cupped her vagina with my hand, ran a finger along its soaking folds. "Yes, you're wet," I said. "But you can't feel it?"

She shook her head as I pulled my hand back. "No, nothing down there. Even if I had a boyfriend, it wouldn't do anything for me. Doesn't mean I still don't..." She grimaced, searched for words. "I have all the usual urges. I just don't have anywhere to put them."

"Me too," I said.

"Yeah, right."

"No, I mean it. I hate sex. I do. I hate being touched, I hate it when they put their things in me. Maybe I don't hate it. But it doesn't do anything for me. And the thing that drives me crazy, you know, is that I... I think about it all the time." I looked down at the floor.

"Apparently you have a thing for pimples," she said.

"I have a thing for everything. And everyone." And there it was: my secret, so fervently kept for so many years, blurted out in earnest. Likely because I realized there was no use holding back, I looked up and locked eyes with her. "I think about it all the time about everyone. I can't see people as people. And nothing's off-limits. I've thought about doing the most horrible things to you. I've masturbated to the thought of raping you in the middle of the night."

"I've dreamed of crippling you."

"I know," I said. "I read your diary."

"You what?"

"I read your diary, on your laptop," I said breathlessly. "I read your diary and I think maybe I fell in love with you, you're the only person I know who hates herself as much as I do, but you're not like me, you shouldn't hate yourself like that, you're beautiful and you should know that, you need someone to tell you that you're beautiful and maybe, maybe you need someone to love you and maybe I can do that, I don't know, this is so fucked up, I'm so weird and I'm sorry."

"You can love me," she said suddenly.

"I think I do love you, I don't know. I hated you two hours ago."

"I hated you ten minutes ago," said Vivian.

"I didn't think I loved you until I said it. But I think I do. Is that weird?"

"I am like you," said Vivian. "You said I'm not, but I am. I'm not exactly like you, but I am and you can love me, just tell me what happens next."

"What happens next...?"

"You've kissed my face," said Vivian. "You took off my shirt and my bra and you've sucked my pimples like crazy, you've sucked them until they hurt. So what do you do to me next?"

And so I told her. Though I didn't touch her, though I didn't do any of the things that I said I was doing to her, that day in the kitchen she had her first orgasm.

We are an unconventional couple. Though we sleep in the same bed, we're rarely naked and we almost never touch each other in a sexual way. Our sex life is completely verbal. We'll share fantasies with one another. We almost never talk about ourselves, but always about other people, people we feel safe using and "doing" perverted things to. (I don't want to use her. Not my Viv.) It will sometimes take hours, but the two of us can bring one another to climax without any physical sensation at all. In fact, I can't even remember the last time I masturbated.

Her family doesn't like me, obviously. Their animosity towards me only increased when Vivian moved in with me. We endure them for holidays but we're always the last to arrive and the first to leave.

I don't think they hate me because I was first with Slater and then with his sister, or even because I "turned Vivian gay". I think they hate me because I chose Viv over Slater. That I chose the broken one over the good one, that I chose the family embarrassment over the family pride.

Viv doesn't miss them.

Viv seems to be better. Seems to hate herself less. Or, if it hasn't changed, she's gotten better at hiding it. That worries me sometimes.

But I think she's happy. I think I make her happy.

I still think about sex all the time. I still feel guilty about some of the things I think about. It's still hard to look someone in the eye the day after I've used them. I still hate myself. And I still wish I was normal.

But sometimes, when I look at her, I feel something quiet and soft inside of me, something just beyond my ability to name it. Sometimes, I don't hate myself quite as much as I used to. Sometimes, I'm content to be who I am, without apologies, without explanations.

That's what she does for me. That's what I try to do for her.

I think that's love.

But sometimes, when I look at her, I feel something quiet and soft inside of me, something just beyond my ability to name it. Sometimes, I don't hate myself quite as much as I used to. Sometimes, I'm content to be who I am, without apologies, without explanations.

That's what she does for me. That's what I try to do for her.

I think that's love.

Dedicated, without irony, to my lovely and amazing spouse, Mary.

With thanks to my partner-in-crime Jamie Rosen, who came up with this whole crazy Eightfold thing in the first place, and whose own WEIRD ROMANCE inspired DOOMED and KINKY.

Made in the USA
Lexington, KY
24 July 2010